## "Ah, Titania by moonlight."

Natasha stiffened as she heard Luke's voice in her ear.

Too disturbed by his presence to guard her words, she said acidly, "Well, you're certainly no Oberon, but we're definitely ill met." She had been trying to avoid him, but now here he was beside her, making her skin tingle.

"Are you cold?"

He must know that she was not, because his fingers were tracing the line of her collarbone, stroking it almost, lazily and carelessly, ignoring her attempt to move away from him.

"You're quite an actress," he murmured. "Today, the epitome of a cool and demure young lady." His voice mocked her. "And yet the last time we met, you were the epitome of an eager wanton, a woman of passion and desire."

**PENNY JORDAN** was constantly in trouble in school because of her inability to stop daydreaming—especially during French lessons. In her teens, she was an avid romance reader, although it didn't occur to her to try writing one herself until she was older. "My first half-dozen attempts ended up ingloriously," she remembers, "but I persevered, and one manuscript was finished." She plucked up the courage to send it to a publisher, convinced her book would be rejected. It wasn't, and the rest is history! Penny is married and lives in Cheshire.

Penny Jordan's striking mainstream novel, *Power Play*, quickly became a *New York Times* bestseller. She followed that success with *Silver*, a story of ambition, passion and intrigue.

Her latest blockbuster, *The Hidden Years*, lays bare the choices all women face in their search for love.

## Books by Penny Jordan

HARLEQUIN PRESENTS
1353—SO CLOSE AND NO CLOSER
1369—BITTER BETRAYAL
1388—BREAKING AWAY
1404—UNSPOKEN DESIRE
1418—RIVAL ATTRACTIONS
1427—OUT OF THE NIGHT

HARLEQUIN SIGNATURE EDITION
LOVE'S CHOICES
STRONGER THAN YEARNING

Don't miss any of our special offers. Write to us at the following address for information on our newest releases.

Harlequin Reader Service
P.O. Box 1397, Buffalo, NY 14240
Canadian address: P.O. Box 603,
Fort Erie, Ont. L2A 5X3

# PENNY JORDAN

## game of love

**Harlequin Books**

TORONTO • NEW YORK • LONDON
AMSTERDAM • PARIS • SYDNEY • HAMBURG
STOCKHOLM • ATHENS • TOKYO • MILAN

Harlequin Presents first edition March 1992
ISBN 0-373-11442-7

Original hardcover edition published in 1990
by Mills & Boon Limited

GAME OF LOVE

# CHAPTER ONE

'TASHA, I think I'm going to need your help.'

'What, again?' Natasha Lacey queried humorously, looking up from her work to smile at her cousin. 'What is it this time? Another crisis over the bridesmaids' dresses? If you want my honest opinion, my love, you're never going to make your Richard's sister look anything other than the little dumpling she is. Poor girl. I can well remember what it feels like to be fourteen, chubby and detesting every female in the world who isn't.'

'When you add to that the fact that she virtually worships Richard, it's no wonder that she isn't exactly overjoyed about your marriage.'

'No, it isn't Sara...not this time,' Emma Lacey interrupted hastily. 'Nothing so simple. I only wish it were.'

Natasha's frown deepened. Three years her own junior, Emma had always been more like her sister than her cousin. They had lived in the same small cathedral city all their lives, their parents close friends as well as relatives, both of them glad to have a peer with whom to share the burdens of growing up.

Perhaps because she was the elder, she had always been the calmer, the more logical of the two of them, her emotions and moods controlled and

5

predictable where Emma's were subject to wild variations and swings.

In the family it was tacitly acknowledged that the death of Emma's father when she was fifteen years old had to have been the cause of the sudden wild streak which had then developed in her behaviour—a wild streak which had led her into scrape after scrape, some of them so serious that they had led to a rift developing between the two cousins. Emma, bored and rebellious, had insisted on leaving school at sixteen, while Natasha had gone on to university, calmly and determinedly working her way towards the qualifications she needed while Emma had played her way around the world.

However, if Emma had been a little wild, that part of her life was behind her now, and no one could be more pleased than she was herself that she had fallen in love with Richard Templecombe.

It was true that the Templecombes were not perhaps as happy with the match as Emma's family. For one thing, the Laceys were not and never had been part of the ecclesiastical life of the city, and even though both families had lived there for several generations they inhabited two very different worlds. The Laceys represented commerce and worldliness, the business which the first Jasper Lacey had established on the outskirts of the city over seventy years before being, after the church, the largest employer in the area. The Templecombes, on the other hand, prided themselves on being above such materialistic things as commerce. Their connections with the cathedral and the church went back even further than the

Laceys' connection with the city. Richard's father was dean of the cathedral, he and Richard's mother acknowledged leaders of local ecclesiastical society, and it was generally accepted that, one day, hopefully Richard would follow in his father's footsteps.

A thought struck Natasha and her heart sank. The wedding was less than a week away now, but her sudden fear had to be expressed. 'You haven't... you're not having second thoughts, are you?' she asked.

Emma shook her head and gulped. 'No, I'm not... but Richard probably will, once Luke tells him what I've done.'

'Luke?' Natasha questioned her, snapping off a thread with expert care, and frowning over the repair she had just completed. It seemed ironic that, having spent all those years qualifying and then travelling the world as an embryo news reporter, she should suddenly discover when she was twenty-five years old that the place she really wanted to be was here in this quiet cathedral town, and the thing she really wanted to do was to work with the rich fabrics and embroideries of that world.

She was establishing quite a name for herself now. A couple of prestigious magazines mentioning the quality of her stock, and the sudden demand for fabrics more suitable for the refurbishment of the ancient piles now being acquired by the migrant tide escaping from London, had helped—as had the fact that she had been able to bully her father into expanding the range of ecclesiastical fabrics the company produced so that they had a more general appeal.

'Luke?' she repeated encouragingly. 'I don't think . . .'

'He's Richard's father's cousin. You won't know him, but he's a typical Templecombe,' Emma told her tearfully. 'Narrow-minded, bigoted, just waiting for me to do something wrong so that Richard will break our engagement.'

Being used to her cousin's emotional highs and lows, Natasha merely said calmly, 'Emma, Richard is twenty-seven years old, and quite plainly besotted with you. I can't imagine what this Luke——'

'You don't understand,' Emma interrupted, and then told her dramatically, 'Luke saw me leaving Jake Pendraggon's house.'

Now Natasha did begin to understand and her heart sank a little, although she didn't allow Emma to see it.

Jake Pendraggon had arrived in the city just over a year ago, as colourful a figure as his name suggested, Cornish by self-adoption rather than actual birth, or so Natasha suspected. Certainly he had cleverly, if not too subtly played up the effect of tanned skin, wildly curling black hair and eyes so blue that she thought he must wear contact lenses.

Certainly anyone knowing Emma as Natasha knew her must have realised immediately that Emma would be drawn to Jake Pendraggon like a lemming to a cliff. Certainly it came as no surprise to Natasha to learn that the acquaintanceship between the two of them had obviously developed into something far more intimate.

She herself had been travelling to Italy, Portugal and Spain for much of the time Jake Pendraggon had been living in Sutton Minster, looking for samples of the kind of cloth she wanted her father's factory to reproduce for her, suitably adapted for a non-ecclesiastical market. Her travels had produced some marvellous fabrics, so rich, so mouth-wateringly desirable that her eyes grew dreamy as she remembered the pleasure of discovering them, of——

'Tasha, you must help me. It was all a mistake—I'd only gone to see Jake to tell him that everything was over between us, that I loved Richard. But he was right in the middle of one of the most important parts of his novel. He begged me to stay and type up his notes for him and we worked all night on them. Nothing else happened. But of course Luke would have to be walking down the close just as I opened Jake's door to leave, and, of course, I would have to be wearing the evening dress I'd had on for our engagement party.' She pulled a face. 'I loved that dress... Richard's mother hated it, of course.'

Natasha brushed aside this incidental chatter and demanded fatalistically, 'You don't mean you went straight from your own engagement party to Jake Pendraggon's house, and were then seen leaving it first thing in the morning by Richard's cousin?'

'He's Richard's father's cousin, but in essence... yes.'

'And you never said a word to Richard... never explained.' Natasha frowned. 'But, Emma, if this Luke didn't say anything to Richard at the time, what on earth makes you think he's going to do so now?'

'I heard Richard's mother talking to him. I'd gone round there to see Sara, and the sitting-room door was open. Neither of them knew I was there. Richard's mother was saying how much she wished Richard were marrying someone more suitable.' Emma pulled a face. 'Well, I already knew she doesn't approve of me, and I'm not bothered about that, but then I heard him—Luke—saying in a sort of sinister way, "Well, you don't know—they aren't married yet. Maybe Richard will have a change of heart," and I knew instantly...'

She paused dramatically while Natasha wrinkled her forehead and asked patiently, 'You knew what?'

'That Luke had been waiting until the last possible minute to tell Richard what I'd done, and I know when he's going to do it—tonight at the pre-wedding party. The one your parents are giving for us.'

'Oh, I'm sure you're wrong,' Natasha tried to comfort her. 'I haven't met this Luke, but I'm sure if he had wanted to tell Richard he would have done so months ago—as you should have done yourself,' she added forthrightly. 'It's still not too late,' she continued more gently, knowing her cousin's stubbornness of old. 'Why don't you simply explain to Richard what happened? After all, if it was as innocent as you say——'

'What do you mean "if"?' Emma demanded belligerently. 'Don't you believe me?'

Natasha sighed faintly. 'Yes, I do,' she confirmed. 'But——'

'Exactly!' Emma pounced. 'And it's that "but" that stops me from telling Richard. Everyone knows that Jake and I went out together a few times that time when Richard and I broke up.' She ignored the ironic look Natasha gave her at her deceptive description of the ragingly public and passionate affair Emma had had with the writer while he was supposedly researching his latest blockbuster. 'But I explained to Richard that if he hadn't got cold feet about loving me I'd never have even looked at Jake.' She ignored the look Natasha gave her and added miserably, 'I know he'd *want* to believe me, but given my reputation and the fact that Luke saw me leaving Jake's house...'

'I *can* see the difficulties,' Natasha admitted. 'You know, you should have explained to Richard right away.'

'I should have but I didn't,' Emma said morosely, 'and now, because of that, Luke is going to tell Richard, and then Richard will break our engagement, and my life will be ruined, unless... you must help me, Tasha. Please...'

'I think the best person to help you is yourself, by confiding in Richard,' Natasha told her severely. 'He *is* an adult, Emma, and I'm sure this Luke whoever he is won't be able to stop Richard from loving and marrying you.'

'You don't know him,' Emma told her starkly. 'He's a typical Templecombe, only worse.'

'Worse?' Natasha questioned. 'How?'

'Well, for a start he's completely anti-women. Oh, not in that way,' she hastened to assure her cousin, when she saw Natasha's expression.

'According to Richard he's had women virtually coming out of his ears, since his early teens. And for all that he's even more strait-laced than Mrs T now. According to Richard there was a time when the family almost disowned him, he was so wild.'

'Well, then, he should sympathise with you,' Natasha murmured, picking up another piece of embroidery and examining it lovingly, wondering how it would look hanging on the wall in her own small house, perhaps over the fifteenth-century oak coffer she had been lucky enough to buy at a local auction.

'Not him,' Emma assured her bitterly. 'He's the original reformed rake. He's already advised Richard that we'd be far better waiting another year to marry, and he's told him that he's not sure that I'm the right wife for him, given his calling. Who says that a vicar's wife has to be like Mrs T?' Emma began indignantly.

'Who indeed?' Natasha agreed *sotto voce*, knowing that if she let her cousin run on for long enough she would eventually run out of steam.

'You will help me, won't you?' Emma pleaded, her face suddenly crumpling with real emotion as she said shakily, 'I couldn't bear to lose Richard now, Tasha. I really couldn't. Before... before we were engaged and we had that row, and I got involved with Jake... well, I thought I *could* live without him, that he was just another man, but it isn't like that. I really do love him. I know he loves me too, but——'

'But you don't think he'll believe you if you tell him what you were doing with Jake Pendraggon.'

'He'd want to, but he *is* only human, and if our situations were reversed... Well, I know how I'd feel if I heard that he'd been seen coming out of an ex-lover's house at that time in the morning.'

'What is it you want me to do?' Natasha asked her. 'Kidnap this Luke and keep him out of sight until after the wedding?' she suggested facetiously.

'Don't be silly,' Emma said severely, making Natasha reflect that her cousin *had* changed a little. Time was when she would very probably have suggested just such an outrageous solution to her present problem. 'No, all I want you to do is to pretend to be me—that is, I want you to pretend that it was *you* Luke saw leaving Jake's house. After all,' she continued, warming to her theme and ignoring the stunned look in Natasha's eyes, 'we *do* look alike. We're both blonde and we both have grey eyes; we're both around the same height—— '

'We're cousins, not twins,' Natasha interrupted her drily, 'and we don't look anything like that similar. I'm taller than you for one thing, and——'

'Tasha, please listen. Luke doesn't know me all that well. He only saw me briefly.'

'He saw you wearing the same dress you had worn for your engagement party,' Natasha reminded her very firmly. 'Emma, love, much as I want to help——'

'No, you don't,' Emma interrupted her bitterly. 'You want to stay nice and safe in your own cosy little world. I bet you think just like Luke really, that I don't deserve someone like Richard. Everyone knows that, if Richard had to marry into our family, Mrs T would have much preferred to have you as a daughter-in-law. After all, before you went off to university you and Richard dated for a while.'

'I like Richard as a person, I'm delighted that the two of you are in love, and as for being like this Luke...' Natasha began, determined to nip any further emotionalism in the bud. 'What exactly does he do, by the way?'

'He's an artist,' Emma told her truculently, totally stunning her. 'He paints landscapes. He's quite well known, apparently.'

'Luke Templecombe? I don't think I've ever heard of him.'

'You won't have done, he uses another name—Luke Freres.'

'Luke Freres? *The* Luke Freres?'

'Tasha, please help me. My whole life's happiness could depend on it,' Emma added theatrically.

'What do you want me to do? Wear a placard tonight saying, "It was me you saw leaving Jake Pendraggon's house, and not Emma"?'

'That's not funny. I just want your permission, if Luke does say anything, to deny it by saying that it wasn't me and that it must have been you. After all, what does it matter to you?' Emma pleaded when she saw her cousin's face. 'It isn't as though there's anyone in your life at the moment.'

'And so *my* reputation doesn't matter, is that it?'

Emma looked cross. 'Oh, for goodness' sake, must you be so old-fashioned? Honestly, Tasha, you're archaic. You must be the only twenty-seven-year-old virgin left.'

'A situation which you want me to claim I tried to rectify via a night in Jake Pendraggon's arms,' Natasha derided, ignoring the jibe. 'Come on, Emma. There might be certain similarities between us, but Luke Freres is an artist. Do you honestly think for one moment he's going to believe he saw me when he saw you?'

'It doesn't matter what *he* believes, only what Richard believes,' Emma told her fiercely. 'But, of course, I should have known you would refuse to help. After all, you don't want to lose your reputation as Miss Pure-and-goody-goody, do you?' she added nastily. 'Oh, no, you'd rather Richard broke our engagement and my heart.'

'Stop being so dramatic. I don't think for one moment that Luke Freres will say anything to Richard. Not at this stage, but in the unlikely event that he does——'

'You'll do it! Oh, Tasha, thank you. Thank you!'

Natasha grimaced. She hadn't been about to volunteer to do any such thing, merely to advise her volatile cousin to put her trust in Richard and tell him the truth, but Emma was on her feet, dancing round the attic workroom of the four-storey building which housed Natasha's home, office and work-place, blowing extravagant kisses at her as she headed for the door.

'You don't know what this means to me. I knew you'd help me. I'm so relieved. Let Luke do his worst—he can't hurt me now. Oh, Tasha, I'm so relieved!'

'Emma, wait,' Natasha protested, but it was already too late.

Her cousin had opened the door and was hurrying downstairs, calling back, 'Can't, I'm afraid, I've got a final fitting for the dress and I'm already late. See you tonight at home.'

'Tasha, where on earth have you been? You know everyone's due at eight. It's half-past seven now.'

Natasha stopped on the threshold of the bedroom which had been hers all the time she was growing up and which she still used whenever she had occasion to stay at Lacey Court overnight.

Emma was standing in the middle of the room, dressed in a fetching confection of satin and lace, delectably designed to show off the prettily tanned curves of her breasts and the slenderness of her thighs in a way that was just barely respectable.

'If you're planning to wear that for dinner, then I think you're making a mistake,' Natasha told her thoughtfully, eyeing the camisole and its matching French knickers consideringly.

Emma grinned at her. 'Don't be silly—as though I would.'

'No? Am I or am I not talking to the girl who appeared at her own eighteenth birthday party wearing a basque and little more than a G-string?'

'That was for a dare,' Emma pouted, 'and, anyway, it was years ago.'

'A millennium,' Natasha agreed drily, adding, 'But, if you don't want Richard's parents to catch you wearing such a fetching but highly inappropriate outfit, I suggest you go back to your own room and finish getting dressed.'

'Not yet. I wanted to see you first, and besides, my dress is silk and will crease if I sit down in it. Listen, I've been thinking—tonight you'd better wear your hair like mine, and if you could wear this as well...'

She reached behind her back and lifted something off the bed, holding it up in front of her.

'That's the dress you wore for your engagement party,' Natasha recognised.

'Exactly. I thought if you wore it tonight it would help to convince Luke that it was you he saw and not me.'

'But, Emma, he must know that you were the one wearing it the night you and Richard got engaged. And, besides, it won't fit me. I'm at least five inches taller than you, and two inches wider round the bust.'

'Yes, it will—the top was very loose and skirts are being worn shorter this year.'

'Not that short, and certainly not by me.'

'But you promised,' Emma began, and, to Natasha's exasperation, large tears filled the soft grey eyes so like her own. Even knowing they were crocodile tears and a trick Emma had been able to pull off from her cradle didn't lessen the effect of them. The trouble was that she was *programmed* to respond to them, Natasha decided grimly. Well, this time she was not going to. She would look ridiculous in Emma's dress. Her cousin loved bright colours and modern fashions, but, for some reason, when she and Richard got engaged she had decided

that a sober, sensible little dress in black was bound
to appeal more to his parents than her usual choice
of clothes. No doubt it would have done so if Emma
had stuck to her original decision and not been
swayed by the appeal of a dress which, while it was
black, shared no other virtues in common with the
outfit she had gone out to buy.

True, the dress did have long sleeves, but it also
had a bodice which was slashed virtually to the waist
front and back. True, it was not made of one of
the glittering, eye-popping fabrics Emma normally
chose. Instead it was made of jersey—not the thick,
sensible jersey as worn by Richard's mother and
aunts, but a jersey so fine, so delicate that it was
virtually like silk. Worn over Emma's lissom young
body, it had left no one in any doubt as to its
wearer's lack of anything even approaching the
respectability of proper underwear between her skin
and the dress—a fact which had obviously been
appreciated by the less strait-laced of the male
guests at the party.

It was the kind of dress it took an Emma to carry
off with aplomb and certainly not the kind of dress
Natasha herself would ever dream of wearing. She
was just about to tell Emma as much when her
bedroom door opened and her mother walked in.
Like Emma, she adored clothes, and they adored
her, Natasha acknowledged as she studied her
mother's appearance admiringly. Tall and still very
slim, her mother was wearing pale grey silk, the
simplest of styles and one which Natasha suspected
had had a far from simple price-tag. Diamonds
glinted discreetly in her ears, her hair and make-up

were immaculate; she looked the epitome of the elegant and understated wife of a rich and indulgent man.

She frowned when she saw them, exclaiming, 'Emma, here you are! Darling, you ought to be ready. You'll want to make an entrance. I'll keep everyone in the hall when they arrive and then you'll come downstairs——' She broke off when she saw that Emma was crying. 'What is it?'

'It's Tasha. I wanted her to wear this dress, but she won't. She says she's going to come down to dinner in that awful beige thing she's had for years. You know how we planned everything so that we'd all be in white, grey and black so that the table would look just right with the Meissen dinner service, and now Tasha's going to spoil it all.'

'Really, Tasha,' her mother disapproved. 'You *are* being difficult. You can't possibly wear that dreadful beige.'

'Neither can I wear this,' Natasha told her mother through gritted teeth. Emma was an arch manipulator when she chose. She'd deal with her later, though. 'Remember it—the discreet little number Emma wore for her own engagement party, the dress that virtually gave the archdeacon apoplexy every time Emma leaned forward.'

'Oh, that dress——'

'Tasha's exaggerating,' Emma interrupted. 'It wasn't *that* bad. I only want her to wear it because I want her to look her best. She never makes the most of herself—you've said so yourself. With her hair done like mine instead of screwed up at the back of her head, and this dress . . . It's time people saw how attractive she really is. Do you know, I heard Mrs T actually telling Sara that she needn't worry about how she looked in her bridesmaid's dress because Tasha was bound to look worse, and, while Sara is still young enough to improve, Tasha is virtually on the shelf.'

Natasha closed her eyes and mentally cursed her cousin. If her mother had one fault, it was an almost obsessive antipathy towards Mrs Templecombe, coupled with a desire to upstage her on each and every opportunity—a discreet and very ladylike desire, of course, but nevertheless...

'Oh, did she?' she declared grimly now. 'Emma is right, darling. That dress would look wonderful on you. You're tall enough to carry it off.'

'Am I? And what do you propose I should do about this?' she demanded grittily, picking up the dress and holding it in front of her by the shoulders so that her mother could see the full effect of its plunging neckline.

'It's perfectly decent,' Emma interposed quickly. 'It only looks as though——'

'It's about to fall off,' Natasha finished acidly for her. 'I am *not* wearing this dress.'

'Oh, dear, I'm afraid you're going to have to,' Emma told her, managing to look both guilty and triumphant at the same time. 'You see, I went through your wardrobe when I arrived and...'

Natasha rushed past her and threw open her wardrobe doors, staring at the empty space where her clothes should have been. She always kept a few things here—her formal evening clothes, her gardening wear and one or two other outfits.

As she closed the door she was more angry with Emma than she had ever been in her life. 'I am not wearing that dress, Emma,' she told her icily. 'Even it if means staying up here all night,' she added fiercely.

'Oh, darling, you can't do that. Think how it would look. Imagine what Richard's mother would say. No, I'm afraid you're going to have to do as Emma says and wear the dress. I'm sure it will look stunning on you.'

'Yes, it will,' Emma agreed eagerly. 'And we've just got time to do your hair.'

'Thank you, Emma, I'm quite capable of doing my own hair,' Natasha told her grimly.

She was trapped and she knew it, but she could cheerfully have murdered her cousin when Emma paused by her bedroom door to remind her dulcetly, 'Remember your promise... If Luke...'

Just for a moment, Natasha was tempted to tell her she had changed her mind, but she didn't. She knew quite well that if Luke Freres did try to make trouble between Emma and her fiancé, she would have to stop him. Emma, for all her flightiness, her giddiness, genuinely did love Richard, and really had toned down her wild behaviour as she tried to conform to the standards expected by Richard's family.

Privately Natasha thought that, the sooner Richard and Emma were free of the constraint of Richard's family, the more chance of success their marriage would have. It was fortunate indeed that Richard's first parish was so very far away in Northumberland, where there would be no risk of criticism and interference from his mother. Given the chance, Natasha suspected, Emma would make a very good, if somewhat unorthodox vicar's wife. She genuinely cared about people and understood them, which was more than anyone could ever say for Mrs Templecombe, who expected everyone to live up to the same impossibly high standards as herself.

Twenty minutes later, as the first guests arrived, Natasha stood despairingly in front of her bedroom mirror wondering if she was out of her mind.

She had washed her hair, and blown it into the same stylish bob in which Emma wore hers, although minus the raffish spiky fringe which Emma adopted. With her hair worn in this style she acknowledged that there *was* a fleeting resemblance between Emma and herself, if one discounted the disparity in their heights.

Yes, the hair was all right, but as for the dress...

On, it looked even worse than she had expected. The hem finished at least a couple of inches above her knees, the deep *décolleté* Vs at the front and back of her bodice somewhere that fell just short of her waist. Cleverly sewn into the front of the dress were two pieces of soft shaping which allowed the observer to entertain himself while imagining that the slightest movement of her torso was likely to expose far more of her obviously naked breasts than merely the cleavage between them, yet ensuring that such a sartorial disaster was simply not possible, so that she could not claim as she had intended that she could not wear the thing for fear of disgracing them all by baring her chest to the entire assembled Templecombe clan—something her mother, whose taste was very sharp-edged, would never have allowed.

'Oh, you're ready, then.'

Natasha swung round, her appearance forgotten as she stared at her cousin. Emma was wearing something that looked as though it had been designed for a prim little puritan; grey silk with a huge white collar and cuffs and a delicate bell-shaped skirt that made her look fragile and delicate.

'I've brought you these,' Emma told her. 'Black, silk stockings and satin shoes. I know you don't have any.'

Gritting her teeth, Natasha threatened, 'I don't know why I'm letting you get away with this, Emma. You had it all planned, didn't you? I look like the original scarlet woman, a fitting contrast to my demure little cousin.'

'No, you don't. You look stunning,' Emma told her flatly, and a little wistfully. Her cousin would much rather be wearing the black dress than the grey, Natasha recognised, humour coming to her rescue, while she would have felt much more at home in Emma's puritan outfit.

'Your mother chose this for me. She said it was bound to create a good impression.'

'Oh, it will,' Natasha agreed humorously. 'Pity she got her faiths mixed up, though. As I recall there never was much love lost between the *aficionados* of the high church and the Plymouth brethren.'

She saw that she had lost her cousin and sighed a little. 'All right, I'll wear your dress, Emma, but only...only because you haven't given me any option, and only because I realise how important it is to you that Richard's family accept you, although you know I suspect that Mrs T would respect you far more readily if you stood out against her and were your own person. Richard loves you for yourself, you know. If he'd wanted a carbon copy of his mother he'd have chosen——'

'Louise Grey. Yes, I know that, but his mother doesn't. She's still convinced that a miracle is going to happen between now and the wedding day, and that Richard is going to open his eyes and realise that it's Louise he loves and not me. And with that beast Luke to help her... If you'd been at the engagement party and seen the way he looked at me...'

'In this? Come on, Emma, be your age. Any man——'

'No, not that kind of way,' Emma interrupted her irritably. 'He looked at me...as though...as though I were a bad smell under his nose. Horrid man. You weren't there...you don't know.'

Natasha had missed the engagement party because she had been away on business, persuading a very difficult and jealous Italian manufacturer to allow her father to reproduce some of his designs for the English market.

'Look, I'll have to go down in a minute. I am grateful to you, Tasha. I don't know what I'd have done if you hadn't offered to help.'

'Offered?' Natasha protested indignantly, but Emma was already closing the door behind her.

# CHAPTER TWO

SHE had never liked wearing stockings, Natasha reflected crossly—a fact which Emma had obviously remembered, since she had supplied her with a suspender belt as well as the impossibly fine black silk hosiery she was now wearing. And as for the height of these heels . . . She felt as though she were perched on stilts, towering above all the other women present.

Was it just her own self-conscious awareness of how very much more provocative the dress was than anything she would personally have chosen to wear that made her feel as though she were the cynosure of all eyes, or was it just because she was taller than Emma that she felt that the dress, startling enough when Emma had worn it, on her was not so much teasingly sensual as a direct and flamboyant statement of availability?

She had never in the space of one short half-hour collected so many admiring male glances nor so many disapproving female ones, nor was it an experience she would want to repeat, she decided irritably after she had fended off the fourth attempt of one of Richard's ancient uncles to detach her from the rest of the guests.

'I see Uncle Rufus has been making a play for you,' Emma commented teasingly as she came up to her.

25

'At his age, he ought to know better,' Natasha retaliated acidly, and then added, 'And don't think I haven't realised exactly why you blackmailed me into wearing this...this garment, Emma. With you dressed as though butter wouldn't melt in your mouth and me looking like the original scarlet harlot——'

'In black,' Emma interposed dulcetly and then giggled. 'I can't wait to see Richard's face when he arrives and sees us. He's been delayed and he won't be here until after dinner. He'll be bringing Luke with him.' She twisted her engagement ring nervously with her fingers. 'You won't let me down, will you, Tasha? I couldn't bear to lose Ricky—not now. I never thought I'd ever feel like this. I never imagined I could ever become so emotionally dependent on anyone. It frightens me a little bit.'

Natasha's stern expression softened. 'I'm sure Luke Freres doesn't have any intention of trying to come between you, but I won't go back on my word, Emma. Even though I positively hate you for making me wear this appalling outfit. Stockings as well, and you know how much I loathe them.'

'Really?' Emma giggled again, giving her a coy look. 'Men adore them. Richard said——' She broke off and groaned. 'Oh, no, here's Mrs T bearing down on us, I'm off.'

'Coward,' Natasha whispered after her, as Emma adroitly whisked herself out of the way, leaving Natasha to face Richard's mother alone.

'Well, Natasha, this is a surprise,' Mrs Templecombe said critically as she frowned at her.

'We don't expect to see *you* wearing that kind of outfit.'

Natasha had never particularly cared for the dean's wife, although she had never attracted her criticism in the same way as Emma. That was the trouble about living in a small place where you had spent all your life. You knew everyone, and everyone knew you and felt free to air their opinions and views of your behaviour—even when you were long past the age when such views were welcome or necessary.

'Anyway, isn't that the dress Emma wore when she and Richard became engaged? I told her then it was most unsuitable.'

'Which is why she passed it on to me,' Natasha told her evenly. Much as she herself might sometimes disapprove of Emma's behaviour, she was not going to aid and abet Mrs Templecombe in criticising her cousin.

'Well, I must say I'm surprised to see you wearing it.'

'I'm a career woman, Mrs Templecombe, and setting up my own business doesn't allow me either the time or the money to waste on clothes shopping. To tell the truth I was grateful to Emma for offering to lend it to me.'

A lie if ever there was one, but Richard's mother seemed to accept it at face-value.

'Yes. I must say it was rather adventurous of you to open your own shop, and selling ecclesiastical fabrics to the general public.'

Her face suggested that what Natasha was doing was somehow or other in rather poor taste, making

Natasha itch to say rebelliously that the cloth wasn't sanctified, but instead she contented herself with murmuring, 'Well, they're very much in vogue at the moment, and are being snapped up by people with a taste for traditional fabrics who can't afford to buy the original antiques.'

'Ah, there you are, Lucille. Such a pity there isn't time to show you round the gardens before dinner. I particularly wanted to show off the new section of the double border. We've planted up part of it with a mixture of old-fashioned shrub roses, underplanted with campanula and a very pretty mallow.'

Smiling gratefully at her aunt, Natasha adroitly excused herself, marvelling on the unsuitability of some people's names as she walked away. Surely only the most doting of parents could have chosen to name Richard's mother Lucille. Her second name was Elsie, which she much preferred and which everyone apart from Emma's mother was wise enough to use.

If her aunt and mother were nothing else, they were certainly marvellous and inspired cooks, Natasha admitted when the main courses had been removed from the table and the sweet course brought in.

Another bone of contention between the ecclesiastical fraternity and her own family was the large pool of temporary domestic assistance her mother and aunt could call upon from the wives and daughters of some of the factory's employees, who would cheerfully and happily help out on the domestic scene when necessary. This willingness to do such work stemmed as much from her aunt's and mother's treatment of those who supplied such help as from the generous wages paid by her father, both women being keen believers in the motto 'Do unto others...'

It was a constant source of friction at the deanery and elsewhere in the cathedral close that they, who were frequently called upon to involve themselves in all manner of entertaining, were hard put to it to get so much as a regular cleaner, but then, with Mrs Templecombe to set the tone for the whole of the cathedral close, it was not perhaps surprising that they would find it difficult to hold on to their domestic help.

His mother, as Richard cheerfully admitted, had been born into the wrong century and adhered to an out-of-date and sometimes offensive policy of 'us and them'.

As it was a warm evening, once the meal was over the guests were free to wander through the drawing-room's french windows, on to the terrace overlooking the gardens. Natasha escaped there, avoiding the fulsome compliments of her coterie of elderly admirers, and the fierce glares of their wives.

Really, she reflected, as she stood breathing in the scented night air, she had had no idea that being a siren involved such hard work. It was just as well she had no ambitions in that direction.

In the distance, the cathedral bells tolled the hour. The bells were one of the first things she missed when she was away from home. Her little house inside the city was almost in the shadow of the bell tower, and she had grown used to timing her telephone calls to avoid clashing with their sonorous reminder of the passing hour.

However, much as she loved the cathedral, much as she enjoyed the pomp and ceremony of its religious feast days, much as she adored the richness of its fabrics and embroideries, if she ever got married she would want a simple ceremony: a simple, plain church, flowers from her aunt's garden, a few special friends and only her very closest family.

She didn't envy Emma her big wedding in the least, and she certainly did not envy her all the palaver that went with it. What she did envy her in a small corner of her mind was having found someone she loved and who loved her in return. Sighing to herself, Natasha wondered if she was ever going to totally grow out of what she now considered to be a silly, immature yearning for that kind of oneness with another human being.

She had lived long enough now to recognise that marriage was a far from idyllic state, one that should only be entered into after a long, cool period of appraisal and consideration, and preferably only if one had developed nerves of steel and was devoid of all imagination; and yet, even though she knew all this, there were still nights like tonight when the soft, perfumed air of the garden led her into all manner of impossible yearnings...

She slipped off her shoes and walked to the edge of the terrace away from the haunting scent of the roses climbing on the wall, and it was while she was standing there, looking out across the shadowed garden, that she heard a familiar voice exclaiming,

'Emma, darling, there you are!' and felt a pair of male hands on her shoulders.

Immediately she turned round, saying wryly, 'Sorry, Richard, I'm afraid it's not Emma, but Natasha.'

'Tasha? Good heavens!'

At another time, the disbelief in his voice would have amused her, but now for some reason it merely served to underline her own aloneness.

'For a moment I thought... You and Emma normally look so different. I'd never have mistaken the two of you. I... You look so different...'

Richard faltered into the kind of silent eloquence of a man who had confidently flung himself off the top of the highest diving-board, only to discover that the pool below him was empty of water, but Natasha took pity on him and said drily, 'Luckily for you, I'm prepared to take that as a compliment, even if it was a rather back-handed one. I think you'll find Emma's in the drawing-room talking to your mother.'

'Tasha, I'm sorry. I didn't mean...'

'I know you didn't,' she agreed wryly, and then added severely, 'Just don't do it again.'

'I suppose I'm so much in love with Emma that I can't think of anyone else. I saw you out here wearing her dress—— Why *are* you wearing it, by the way?' he asked awkwardly. 'I mean, it isn't your sort of thing at all, is it?'

'Oh, isn't it?' she asked quizzically, watching him flush uncomfortably, irritated without knowing why that he should automatically assume that she didn't have either the ability or the desire to be seen as a sensual woman.

In fact, she was so engrossed in the shock of discovering that she could feel such illogical irritation
that she didn't realise they weren't alone until he
looked abruptly away from her and said eagerly,
'Luke, come and meet Emma's cousin, Natasha.
Natasha, I'd like to introduce you to my, or rather
my father's cousin, Luke.'

Without knowing why, as she turned round
Natasha felt both vulnerable and nervous.

The man walking along the terrace towards her
had the familiar Templecombe features of a tall,
athletic frame, good bone-structure and a shock of
dark hair, but in him some rogue genes had added
features which neither Richard nor his father possessed, she recognised uneasily.

Whereas the most common expression on the
faces of Richard and his father was one of benign,
almost unworldly kindness, on this man's face was
an expression of hard cynicism; his eyes, unlike
Richard's, weren't brown, but a light, pale colour
which seemed to reflect the light, masking his
expression. He was taller than Richard, and
broader, somehow suggesting that beneath his suit
his body was packed with powerful muscles and
that it had been used in far more vigorous and dangerous ways than playing a round of golf. Natasha,
who had never in her life experienced the slightest
curiosity or arousal at the thought of the nude male
body, suddenly found herself wondering helplessly
if the dark hair she could glimpse so disturbingly
beneath the crisp whiteness of his shirt cuff grew
as vigorously and as masculinely on other parts of

his body, and if so what it would be like to feel its crispness beneath her fingertips.

She stiffened as though her body had received a jolt of electricity, and heard him saying evenly and without any inflexion in his voice at all, which somehow made it worse, 'Emma's cousin. Ah, yes, I thought I recognised the dress.'

'Yes, so did I. In fact I thought for a moment that Tasha was Emma.'

'Really?'

Natasha watched, fascinated, as the dark eyebrows rose indicating polite disinterest, and then said hurriedly, 'I think we'd better go in. Emma will be wondering——'

'If you've borrowed her fiancé as well as her dress,' the cynical voice suggested, causing Natasha to grit her teeth and force back the sharp retort springing to her lips. He might move in the kind of circles where people swapped lovers as easily as they changed clothes, but if he thought that he could come here and insult her by suggesting... But what was the point in quarrelling with him? As a painter he might be worthy of her admiration, she thought angrily as she stalked past both men, realising too late that she had not retrieved her shoes, but as a man...

'Won't you need these?'

Seething, she turned round to discover that he was holding her shoes. Damn the man; he must have eyes like a hawk. Of course, as a painter he would be used to monitoring every tiny detail. Her heart started to jump erratically as he came towards her. His wrist and hand were tanned a rich brown, and as she put out her own hand to retrieve her shoes she noticed how pale and somehow delicate her own skin looked against his, how fragile her wrist-bones—so fragile that, if he were to curl his fingers around her wrist, he could break it as easily as he might snap a twig.

She gulped and swallowed, furious with herself for her idiotic flight of fantasy, almost snatching the shoes from him with an ungracious mutter of thanks.

Richard, keen to find Emma, had already gone inside, and she wished that his cousin would follow suit, she decided resentfully as she put the shoes on the terrace and then started to step into them.

As she slipped on the first one, the heel wobbled alarmingly and she kicked the other shoe over. Cursing the uneven paving of the terrace, she started to bend down to pick it up and then tensed as Luke Templecombe said coolly, 'Allow me.' He was already holding the shoe and there was nothing she could do other than grit her teeth and stoically concede defeat as he suggested mockingly, 'I think it would be much simpler if you put your hand on my shoulder to steady yourself. The ground here is very uneven—hardly suitable for this kind of footgear, but then when ever did a woman consider suitability of prime importance when choosing what to wear?'

Natasha opened her mouth to deny his unfair comment, and then closed it again, her whole body going into shock as she felt his fingers close round her ankle.

'Silk stockings,' she heard him murmur, and then, unbelievably, his hand travelled up her leg, resting briefly on her knee before travelling expertly along her thigh, stopping on a level with the hem of her skirt.

For almost thirty seconds Natasha was too mortified to speak, to do anything other than tremble in furious indignation. When her paralysed vocal cords were working again, to her intense chagrin all she could manage was a very mundane and choked, 'How dare you? What do you think you're doing?'

'I thought I was accepting the none too subtle invitation I was being given,' he told her laconically. 'No woman who wears black silk stockings and that kind of dress is doing so because she *doesn't* want to be looked at and touched.'

Natasha was furious.

'How dare you?' she repeated, almost stammering in her rage. 'I suppose you're the kind of man who believes that women are never raped— that when they say no, they always mean yes. For your information, I am wearing this dress and these stockings, not for the disgusting reasons you have just suggested, but because——'

She stopped then, realising that she could not tell him exactly why she was dressed as she was. She looked wildly at him and saw that he was still watching her with cynical amusement, waiting for her to go on, and instead of completing her sentence she said thickly, 'Oh, go to hell!' and stormed rudely past him, ignoring the mocking laughter that followed her, so upset that she was physically trembling, that she wanted nothing more than to rip the dress from her skin and to consign it and the stockings to the fire, and then to bury her head under her bedclothes and give way to the relief of a prolonged bout of tears.

No one...no one had ever infuriated her like that, nor insulted her like that...no one had ever made her feel so many confusing or violent emotions within such a short space of time.

Emma had been right; the man was loathsome, abhorrent, dangerous...

Very dangerous, she acknowledged, giving a tiny shiver. Very, very dangerous indeed.

## CHAPTER THREE

IT WAS the dress, Natasha told herself shakily half an hour later on her way back downstairs from her bedroom, to which retreat she had escaped to recover her poise and pull herself together.

It *had* to be the dress. It couldn't be anything else. Surely nothing in her manner could possibly have given him the impression that she actually wanted... She swallowed hard, furious with herself for the shaky, nervous feeling invading the pit of her stomach—the feeling that said that underneath her anger, underneath her shock and fury had lain a very discernible and disturbing quicksilver flash of pleasure in the way his fingers had brushed her skin.

As she paused just inside the open drawing-room door, taking in the normality of the scene in front of her, it seemed impossible to believe it had actually happened.

The trouble with you, my girl, she told herself shakily, is that you're too used to men regarding you as being as sexless as an elderly maiden aunt. Where's your sense of humour? No doubt scores of women would have been highly flattered by his approach.

As she skirted the room, keeping a wary eye out for Luke Templecombe and wondering what on earth Richard's mother was likely to say if she told her what had happened, she saw her cousin and

Richard standing hand in hand gazing foolishly into one another's eyes, the epitome of a young couple in love.

'Stopped sulking, have you?'

She froze as the softly spoken words just brushed the tip of her ear. Intense waves of sensation washed right down over her body from that spot to the tips of her toes, making her want to curl them in protest.

She just—*just*—managed to stop herself from turning round, and instead gritted with acid sweetness, 'I wasn't aware that I was. If you'll excuse me, I must go and help my mother.'

'Not just yet.'

This time she couldn't prevent herself from swinging round as she felt the now familiar sensation of those lean fingers clamping her wrist and holding her captive.

She panicked immediately, hissing furiously at him, 'Will you let me go? What is it with you? Does it turn you on to...to force yourself on women?'

The smile he gave her was feral, making her shiver inwardly.

'Does it give *you* a thrill to force yourself on men—visually, at least?'

Natasha discovered that she had clenched her fingers into a fist; she also discovered that nothing would have given her greater pleasure than to hit the hard male face staring into her own with the open palm of her hand—a discovery which shocked her into stunned silence. No man had ever made her feel like this...infuriated her like this...insulted her like this.

'For your information, I am wearing this dress because *I* happen to like it,' she lied flagrantly.

'Do you, or is it the sensation of male eyes following your every movement that you like? Come on, be honest—no woman wears a dress like that unless she wants a man to look at her and be sexually aware of her.'

There was nothing she could say. In her heart of hearts, she knew what he was saying was perfectly true.

'Admittedly I suppose it's possible that a naïve woman might perhaps foolishly wear such a dress for one particular man, forgetting in the heat of her—er—desire that something intended to arouse only one particular male was likely to have the same effect on every male who sees her in it.'

Natasha stared at him and then said huskily, 'If that's meant to be an apology——'

'It isn't,' came back the crisp response. 'I don't consider I have anything to apologise for.'

He had released her wrist and as she stepped back from him, rubbing her wrist as she glared at him, even though the pressure he had exerted had not hurt her at all, he bent his head and murmured softly against her ear, 'Think yourself fortunate it was only your leg I touched. The combination of that black silk jersey and the knowledge that you aren't wearing a damn thing underneath it tempts far more than a man's gaze to linger on your breasts. Personally, I've always considered that a woman with anything over a thirty-two B chest should never be seen in public without her bra, but I must admit that you've gone a long way to change my mind, sexually if not aesthetically, although I would suggest that such a cleavage *is* rather gilding the lily; a simple high neckline would have been just as alluring and far more subtle.'

Natasha gaped at him in disbelief.

'You look like a little girl who's suddenly seen her grandmother turn into the wicked wolf,' he taunted her. 'Surely you knew the effect your outfit was going to have?'

Out of the corner of her eye, Natasha saw Mrs Templecombe watching them frowningly. The last thing she wanted was for Richard's mother to realise how upset she was, and so, ignoring his remark, she said brittly, 'Richard and Emma make a good couple, don't they? I think they'll be very happy together.'

'Do you?' He gave her a sardonic look. 'Personally I'd have thought them exceptionally ill suited.' He saw the outrage darken her eyes and added cruelly, 'Your cousin has to be one of the most light-minded females I have ever come across, while Richard is destined to be a Templecombe in the same mould as his father and his before that. He's a dedicated, very serious young man, who at the moment is infatuated by a pretty face and a willing body. Do you honestly want me to believe that they have the remotest chance of happiness together? I give them six months or less before she's as bored as hell with playing at being the vicar's wife and is looking around for the kind of diversion I caught her enjoying last year—on the very night she and Richard announced their engagement.'

Natasha discovered that her heart was thumping frantically, as though she had suddenly and frighteningly come face to face with something she found dangerous. And this man *was* dangerous, she recognised inwardly, both to Emma's happiness and to her.

'What exactly are you trying to say?' she asked him unevenly.

He gave her a long look.

'Oh, come on, don't tell me you don't know about your cousin's premarital fling with Jake Pendraggon. I myself saw her leaving his house the very morning after she and Richard announced their engagement.'

As she looked into his face, any thoughts of trying to explain, to make him understand vanished, and she heard herself saying coldly, 'I think there must be some misunderstanding...'

'*I* don't think so—the facts spoke for themselves. Facts which I suspect Richard remains ignorant of, poor fool. And if she was unfaithful to him on the very night they got engaged... She was wearing that dress you've got on tonight.'

Without stopping to think, Natasha drew herself up to her full height and lied determinedly.

'You mean you *think* you saw Emma. In actual fact *I* was the one you saw. I arrived home too late to attend the party. I rang Jake and he invited me to go round. Emma had come home by then. She knew I didn't want to drive back to my own place and get changed, so she offered to lend me her dress. Jake likes his women to look...'

'Available?' he supplied silkily for her.

\* \* \*

'Hello, Luke. You two certainly seem deep in conversation.'

Both of them swung round at the sound of Emma's voice. Richard was standing beside her and, as though she had been fabricating lies all her life, Natasha said smoothly, forcing a light laugh, 'Emma, you'll never guess what—Luke saw me leaving Jake's house last year, after your engagement party, and he actually thought I was you.'

Somehow or other Emma managed to look not just shocked but affronted as well. 'I did help Jake out with some research on his book,' she said stiffly, 'and there was some silly gossip at the time. I think you found it quite amusing, didn't you, Tasha? Are you still in touch with Jake?'

'No,' Natasha told her curtly, suddenly very annoyed with her cousin. It was one thing to help Emma out of a difficult situation; it was quite another for her cousin to openly brand her as Jake Pendraggon's lover.

'Richard tells me you won't be able to make it for the wedding, Luke,' Emma was saying.

'No, I'm afraid not. I'm tied to a commission I accepted some time ago.'

It was said so urbanely and with so little regret that Natasha couldn't help reflecting that he was not really sorry to be missing the ceremony at all.

Suddenly she felt so exhausted, so drained that she could barely stand up. The pit of her stomach felt as though it were lined with lead; her head ached and all she really wanted to do was to go somewhere where she could be alone. Excusing herself, she hurried towards the door. Some fresh air might help to clear her head. Not on the terrace this time—that was too public, too visible. No, she could creep out of the back door and wander round her aunt's closed kitchen garden.

In the porch off the kitchen, she hesitated long enough to put on an old pair of trainers and the Barbour jacket her aunt used when she was gardening. She felt cold inside. Cold and empty in some way that made her want to hug her arms round her body.

As she let herself into the kitchen garden through the wooden door, she paused to breathe in the cleansing smell of her aunt's herbs. She wished it might be as easy to cleanse her mind, her soul of the besmirchment it had suffered tonight. It was no use telling herself that Luke Templecombe didn't know the first thing about her, that the woman he had insulted and scorned was not really her at all. She still felt sore, humiliated, defiled...

There was enough light from the moon for her to see the brick paths quite clearly. There was a seat under the wall, framed by an arbour of grapes which her aunt kept out of sentiment, claiming that the fruit they produced was worse than useless. She went and sat down on it, leaning back and closing her eyes, breathing deeply as she tried to unwind. It took her several concentrated minutes of forcing herself to breathe evenly and deeply before she felt she was properly back in control of herself.

That infuriating man. She prided herself on her calm, unflappable nature, but he had well and truly pierced the barrier of her self-control and revealed a woman of emotions and feelings even she had not known existed. Don't think about him, she warned herself as she felt her tension returning, but it was a very difficult mental command to obey when his cynical, vaguely piratical features insisted on forming themselves against the darkness of her closed eyes.

'Ah ... Titania by moonlight.'

The too familiar, drawling voice shocked her into opening her eyes and staring in disbelief as she saw the object of her thoughts standing in front of her.

Too disturbed by his presence to guard her words, she said acidly, 'Well, you're certainly no Oberon, but we're definitely ill met.'

She stood up abruptly, intent on escaping from him just as quickly as she could. He was standing several feet away from her and it should have been easy, but for some reason her feet seemed to be stubbornly glued to the path, while he moved easily and lithely towards her, blocking her exit.

'What *is* it you want?' Natasha heard herself asking breathlessly, helplessly almost, and inwardly she railed against the weakness in her voice, and her folly in asking the question.

He seemed to think so too, because he laughed, a soft, dangerous sound that raised the flesh on her arms, his teeth a brief flash of white in the dimness of the garden.

'Such sweet innocence. You sound about sixteen years old, but it won't wash, my dear. You know exactly what I want.'

He took a step towards her and then another, while she stood there like a transfixed rabbit, unable to move.

When he took hold of her, his hands sliding beneath the heavy fabric of her borrowed Barbour, she shuddered deeply, and, as though he found the sensitive reaction of her flesh intensely satisfying, he murmured against her ear, 'I've been wanting to do this all evening.'

Distantly Natasha was aware of his sliding the heavy jacket off her shoulders, and binding her to him with arms hard with muscles she could feel even through the fabric of their clothes. His head angled towards her, blotting out the moon. Panic attacked her as she suddenly recognised her own foolishness in not escaping earlier. Her mouth had gone dry; her lips felt stiff and cold. She badly wanted to touch them with her tongue, a nervous reaction, and one which she was well aware he would read as intensely provocative. She could see the clear white of his eyes and the light reflective gleam of his iris. She could even see the hard angle of his jaw and the firm curve of his mouth. Soon that mouth would be touching hers... Soon... Was she mad? she wondered in a frantic surge of reality. Had he cast some sort of spell over her, to render her so quiescent and submissive?

His mouth only a breath away from her own, he told her softly, 'I've been wanting to do this all evening, wondering how you would feel and taste.'

'Well, I haven't,' she countered jerkily, trying to pull back from him and escape, but it was too late.

As she turned her head to avoid his kiss, he caught hold of it, sliding his palm along her jaw, imprisoning her so that she couldn't move her head without hurting herself, his voice edged with mockery and cynicism as he told her, 'You're a liar.'

And then he was kissing her—not roughly or cruelly as she had always naïvely imagined men *did* kiss women for whom all they felt was an emotionless physical ache, but with such great subtlety, such instinctive awareness of her own needs and responses that it was as though the whole world had caved in around her, leaving her floating helplessly in a dimension she had never even imagined existed.

The pressure of his mouth moving against her own was at once so caressive, so knowing, so persuasive, that she simply didn't have any defences against it. Despairingly she recognised that, while her mind might not have wanted this intimacy, her body certainly had, and, humiliatingly, he must have been aware of that wanting even though she herself had not.

Helplessly unable to stop herself giving him the response he demanded, she heard him make a small sound deep in his throat, and felt her own flesh thrill in recognition of what it meant. His hand was no longer cupping her face; instead it was caressing her throat, pushing aside the shoulder of her dress so that his fingers could caress the smooth, pale flesh he had revealed.

Even though she could feel the fabric sliding away from her skin, even though she *knew* from the slightly rough contact of his dinner-jacket against her skin that the bodice must have slipped away to reveal her breast, she made no attempt to stop him, no attempt to do anything other than clutch at his shoulders and gasp a tiny sound of shocked arousal as his lips caressed the smooth line of her throat, and his hand slid into the gaping bodice of her dress to completely free both breasts, first to his touch, then to his gaze, and finally to the caress of his mouth.

And now he wasn't either gentle or restrained and, shockingly, in response to the demand of his mouth she felt fierce surges of pleasure and desire wash through her body, so powerful, so compulsive that she cried out in protest when his mouth released one breast before turning to the other, her hands clenching on his shoulders as her newly aroused senses silently urged him to repeat the agonisingly arousing caress.

When he did so, she trembled violently in open response, causing him to linger over the sensitive nub of flesh he was enjoying, before lifting his head to mutter against her mouth, 'You've been driving me crazy with the need to taste you like that all evening, *and* you know it, you little witch. Richard says you have a place of your own near the cathedral. Let me . . .'

It was like being immersed in a bath of icy water. Where she had been swept away by sensations, emotions so totally foreign to her that in his arms nothing had been more important than the pleasure he was giving her, now abruptly she came back to reality and suffered a corresponding surge of self-revulsion.

How many times in the past had she quickly and coldly turned down those men foolish enough to imagine that she could possibly want a sexual relationship with them on the strength of an acquaintance that could be counted only in hours? It was a hazard of that part of her work which involved travelling and buying abroad. Never once had she been even remotely tempted to indulge in that kind of brief sexual thing. It was something she utterly and completely abhorred.

She had always believed that, for her, sexual desire was something she would only experience for someone with whom she was deeply and passionately in love, which was why, as Emma had taunted her earlier, she was still a virgin. And yet now here she was in the garden of her parents' home allowing a man—and not just any man either, but one she had already decided she disliked and distrusted intensely—to caress her so intimately that she had given him the impression that she was ready to go to bed with him.

Perhaps something of her feelings showed in her face, because suddenly he had released her and he now stood watching her . . . waiting.

Quite what would have happened if she hadn't heard her mother calling her name, Natasha wasn't sure. As it was she could only feel immense relief and gratitude that she was saved from making any explanation, from saying anything other than a husky, 'I must go,' before practically running away from him.

It was only later when she was helping her mother to serve coffee and a light supper to their guests that she remembered she had left her aunt's jacket in the garden. She shivered, her face suddenly pale, causing her mother to say anxiously, 'Tasha, are you all right? The last thing we need now is you going down with a summer cold. What on earth were you doing in the garden anyway?'

'I had a headache and wanted some fresh air,' she responded tensely, while she surreptitiously searched the room, unsuccessfully looking for Luke Templecombe.

It wasn't until she saw Emma half an hour later that she discovered he had gone.

'You can relax now,' her cousin told her cheerfully. 'Luke's gone, thank goodness. Oh, and thanks for letting him and Richard think that it *was* you leaving Jake's house.'

'I still think it would have been better for you to tell Richard the truth,' Natasha told her. 'He loves you and I'm sure he'd understand.'

'Not yet,' Emma told her positively. 'He does love me, but I don't think he's sure enough of me yet to believe that I could spend the night with Jake simply working with him. I was right about Luke, wasn't I? He really is horrible. He's fantastic-looking, of course, and a wow with the women according to Richard, but I bet inside he's as cold and hard as ice. I can't see him ever allowing himself to fall in love, can you? Richard says Luke's very anti-marriage—considers it a trap and all that kind of thing. Apparently his parents were very unhappy together, but because his father was a Templecombe there was no question of divorce. They married at the end of the war, and Luke's mother had been in love with someone else. He was killed and so she married Luke's father, but it didn't work out.

'His father died when Luke was fourteen years old. An overdose of sleeping tablets. Accidental death, according to the authorities, but Richard says Luke always believed that he killed himself when he found out that Luke's mother was having an affair with someone else and that she was leaving her husband. He never forgave his mother. He ran away from home when he was sixteen and virtually worked his way around the world. Richard says he feels rather sorry for him—personally I think he's the pits, don't you?'

'He certainly isn't someone I'd like to see a lot of,' Natasha agreed hollowly.

Impossible not to feel some sympathy for the unhappy child he must have been, but he wasn't a child any longer; he was a man—a cruelly cynical and dangerous man. A man who would have taken her to bed simply to ease a physical ache without feeling the slightest degree of liking or respect for her as a human being. She shivered convulsively, and decided grimly that as soon as tonight was over she was going to take Emma's dress, and her stockings and her silly high-heeled shoes and throw the lot of them on the fire, and if Emma ever, ever asked her to do anything to help her again she would most definitely refuse.

'What's wrong?' Emma asked her curiously. 'You look as though you're thinking of murdering someone.'

'Mm . . . would it surprise you to know that that someone is you? Don't ask me for any more favours, Emma. I don't think I could survive it.'

'What? Not even being godmother to our first child?' Emma teased, laughing when Natasha said fervently,

'No... not if he or she is going to inherit your aptitude for getting into trouble.'

# CHAPTER FOUR

'How do I look? Is my veil straight?' Emma asked Natasha anxiously for about the tenth time.

'Yes. It's straight. And you look wonderful,' Natasha assured her firmly and truthfully.

Emma, in her cream silk wedding dress and wearing the veil that had been their grandmother's, was a breathtakingly beautiful bride. Now, as she prepared to leave for the church with Sara, the other bridesmaid, Natasha bent to kiss her cousin's cheek and then picked up the full skirts of her own dress, hurrying Sara out of the room and downstairs.

The soft cream of their dresses with their apricot sashes were almost as lovely in their way as Emma's stunningly beautiful gown, Natasha admitted, pausing briefly to check the neckline of her own in the mirror and adjust its off-the-shoulder puff sleeves.

Thank goodness Luke Templecombe wasn't coming to the wedding. She was still smarting and sore from her run-in with him at the pre-wedding dinner, still too sharply aware of how intensely she had reacted to him.

There had been sighs of relief all round this morning when they had woken to find the sun shining on a perfect summer's day, although as yet none of them had had time to appreciate it as the whole house had been busy with comings and goings from first thing onwards.

The reception was being held here at the house in a marquee which a skilled team of workmen had erected two days ago. Now, firmly ushering Richard's sister ahead of her, Natasha opened the front door and smiled at the driver of their waiting car. Sara was still scowling. Sulking still over Emma's refusal to allow her to wear pink, no doubt, Natasha reflected as she firmly ignored the younger girl's sullenness and remarked on their good luck with the weather.

The ceremony was taking place at the cathedral, of course. Her own father was giving Emma away. As their car drew up and they got out she heard the appreciative murmurs of the onlookers.

'Everyone's arrived,' her mother told her, hurrying up to her. 'Richard doesn't look in the least nervous.'

'Pa is,' Natasha told her with a grin.

Earlier, suddenly and unexpectedly emotional, Emma had hugged her tightly, tears in her eyes as she whispered, 'Thanks for everything, Tasha...and especially for letting that pig Luke think it was you he saw leaving Jake's. Thank goodness he can't come to the wedding. I'd have been like a cat on hot bricks wondering if he was going to stand up and denounce me when they got to that bit, you know, "If any man..."'

'Yes, I know,' Natasha agreed. 'Although I'm sure he'd never have done anything so dramatic. It's not his style. He prefers a more subtle form of cruelty.'

Emma had given her an odd look, started to say something and then stopped, and no wonder. But fortunately she had been too caught up in her own thoughts to ponder too much on the bitterness in Natasha's voice.

Natasha would never, never forget the way he had treated her in the garden. She went hot with fury and chagrin just to think about it . . . just to remember. And underneath that emotion ran another darker, shameful awareness of how frighteningly he had aroused her.

She saw the car arriving with her father and Emma. As Emma climbed out on to the pavement Natasha knew that she was not the only person discovering that her breath had lodged in her throat and that her eyes were unexpectedly misty.

She was just about to hurry forward to help her cousin with her dress when Sara suddenly said excitedly, 'Oh, good, there's Luke! He's made it after all. Wonderful!'

Luke . . . Luke here . . .? Sara had to be wrong. He had said quite firmly that he would not be able to attend. He couldn't just change his mind like that—not without letting anyone know.

For some odd reason Natasha's heart was beating furiously fast. She knew she ought to move, to hurry forward to Emma's side taking Sara with her, and yet her whole body seemed to be held in a state of suspended shock. Sara was calling out Luke's name and waving frantically. All she needed to do was to turn her head . . . just a few inches . . . No one would ever notice . . . and he would be directly in her line of vision.

The mere fact that she wanted to turn her head jolted her back to reality. The man was a barbarian, cruel and feral, for all his cloaking sophistication. She knew...she had felt the sharp claws of his contempt, the savage teeth of his cold desire. She shivered suddenly, reminding herself that this was Emma's day, and that if her cousin knew that Luke was here it might spoil things for her.

Resolutely ignoring the temptation to turn her head, she took hold of Sara's arm and hissed in her ear, 'Not now, Sara. You can talk to Luke later,' and quickly tugged her in Emma's direction.

Fortunately her cousin was so busy worrying about the delicate lace of her veil that she had not had time to look around her. Hopefully, by the time she did, Luke would have disappeared inside the cathedral with the rest of the guests.

For Natasha, the moving simplicity of the wedding service was overshadowed by her knowledge of Luke's presence. Contrary to the fears Emma had expressed earlier, he did not stand up and denounce her, but then Natasha had never thought that he would. No, his denunciations now were all for her, she thought bitterly as the triumphal surge of the wedding march filled the cathedral and the doors were drawn back to admit the hot brilliance of the afternoon sun.

It was over. Emma and Richard were safely married and there was nothing that Luke Templecombe could do about it, no matter how unsuited he might think them.

What she couldn't understand, she decided uneasily, following Emma back down the aisle, was what he was doing here. It had seemed so certain that he could not attend the wedding, and yet here he was.

She had no idea where he was sitting, nor did she intend to look, but Sara's excited 'Luke!' sent prickles of unwanted sensation burning under her skin, drawing her attention instinctively to his tall, dark-suited frame.

For a moment their eyes met and locked. Something dark and challenging flickered in his, setting up a warning pulse at the base of her throat. When she touched her skin there the betraying gesture drew his attention. The sensation of him looking at her was so strong that she could almost feel the heat of his gaze burning her skin, could almost feel the savage possession of his mouth as it fastened over that frightened pulse.

She felt sick, faint, shocked into a maelstrom of panic and fear. And yet why? What was there to fear? What could he possibly do to her here among her friends and family? What could he possibly *want* to do to her? He had come here to see Richard married, that was all. It was insane of her to think she had read in that feral glance he had given her, that challenging clash of their eyes, another darker purpose.

Why on earth would he want to seek her out? He had made his contempt of her all too plain already, and yet she discovered even once she was outside in the warmth of the sun that her skin felt oddly chilled, that her throat was aching with tension and that she was almost visibly trembling.

All around her was the wash of people's voices, congratulations and laughter, people giving instructions as they were shepherded towards the waiting cars.

No photographs were being taken outside the cathedral. It was deemed unseemly and so everyone was waiting for Emma and Richard to leave so that they could make their way back to Lacey Court.

Only when she was safely inside their own car did Natasha feel able to relax. She ached to turn her head and search feverishly to see where Luke was, what he was doing, but she refused to give in to her weakness. It was fear that was making her feel like this, fear and anger, and of course shock...and yet beneath them lay something else— a dangerous, elemental sexual excitement whose existence tore at her pride, at her self-respect.

'Are you OK?'

Sara's unexpected question made Natasha open her eyes and look at her.

'Yes, yes. I'm fine. Why?'

'You look awful,' she was told untactfully. 'Really white and sick. You didn't want to marry Richard yourself, did you?'

'No, of course I didn't,' Natasha told her shortly. 'I've just got a bit of a headache, that's all...'

Her response seemed to satisfy Sara, who immediately changed the subject and said blissfully, 'I'm so glad that Luke's here. He's wonderful. Much nicer than Richard.'

Natasha's mouth twisted cynically.

At her side Sara was still chattering. 'I'm going to make sure he sits next to me. I'll change the place cards——'

'You can't,' Natasha told her sharply, 'You're on the top table, remember.'

Sara was pouting sulkily. 'Well, I don't see that that matters. I suppose Emma has put me next to some ghastly boy.'

'I've no idea,' Natasha told her shortly. Her heart was still pounding at the thought of finding herself on the same table as Luke, and yet why? Why should she feel this... this fear? Antagonism, dislike, resentment... yes, she could understand herself feeling all these emotions, but fear? And fear of what? Surely not of his repeating that savage caress he had bestowed on her before?

The car had stopped. They were home. She could hear Emma's excited voice. As she climbed out of the car, other cars were arriving... Her parents... Richard's family... And there, in the expensive Jaguar saloon, Luke, dark and predatory, and looking just a little alien in some way among the laughing crowd of guests.

Emma had seen him now, her face expressing her indignation as she hissed to her new husband, 'What's he doing here?'

Richard looked puzzled.

'I don't know. He said he wouldn't be able to make it.'

'Well, it's going to put out all the numbers,' Emma told him indignantly.

When Richard looked helplessly at her Natasha stepped in, saying soothingly, 'I'm sure we'll be able to squeeze him in somewhere.' Somewhere as far away from her as possible. 'I'll go and have a word with the caterers.'

She was only too glad of the excuse to get away, to hurry through the house to the kitchen to find the man in charge of the catering team.

'Yes, a place could easily be made at one of the tables,' he assured her, having listened to her question. She lingered for a few more seconds and then reminded herself that she had other duties, that she was Emma's bridesmaid.

When she returned to the garden the photographer was busy with Emma and Richard. She watched them absently, her senses straining to find Luke so that she could keep well away from him, but she wouldn't allow herself to turn her head.

'Ah, Natasha. My dear...'

She smiled automatically at Richard's mother, and then went cold as she saw Luke standing with her.

'I know you've already met Luke. Such a wonderful surprise that he managed to make it for the wedding after all.'

Woodenly, Natasha said nothing, staring fixedly ahead and then gritting her teeth as he seemed deliberately to step into her line of vision.

Her eyes were on a level with his jaw. She could see the rough growth of beard shadowing the clean-shaven flesh.

'Luke, you remember Natasha, Emma's cousin, don't you?'

'But of course... Quite a metamorphosis,' he added softly under his breath, so softly that

Natasha knew only she was meant to hear it. She felt her skin heat with indignation and resentment, and then saw the way he was looking at her. Like a cat at a mousehole.

'Please excuse me,' she said frigidly. 'They'll be waiting to finish the photographs.' Her face still hot, she walked away. How dared he look at her like that—with that cynical half-smile that said that he knew all her secrets, all her vulnerabilities? He knew nothing about her. Nothing at all.

'Not dancing?'

Natasha stiffened as she heard Luke's voice in her ear. She had left the marquee and come outside for a few minutes' respite from the tension of continuously smiling and talking, trying to appear natural while at the same time trying to avoid Luke. And now here he was behind her, making her spine tingle with tension and her body suddenly go hot and weak.

'I wanted a few minutes alone,' she told him pointedly, refusing to turn around. Not because she was afraid to confront him. After all, what had she done? Nothing...

Nothing other than to present him with a totally false impression of herself. An impression that said she was both sexually experienced and sexually available. But dozens of other women must give him that same message; there was nothing particularly remarkable about her... No reason for him to project towards her this aura of male arousal and awareness. He couldn't want her. And she certainly did not want him. And yet...

She shuddered at the shocking, contrary feeling deep inside her, and then flinched as he reached out and touched her bare shoulder.

'Are you cold?'

He must know that she was not, because his fingers were now tracing the line of her collarbone, stroking it almost, lazily and carelessly, ignoring her attempt to move away from him.

'You're quite an actress,' he murmured. 'Today, the cool demure cousin of the bride, the epitome of what women of Richard's mother's generation believe a young lady should be.' His voice mocked her and then dropped to a harder, dangerous tone as he added, 'And yet the last time we met you were the epitome of an eager wanton, a woman of passion and desire.'

'I must go.'

How weak her voice sounded. How uncertain and hesitant, faintly breathless and nervous—not as she would have wanted it to sound at all.

'Not yet ... No one will miss us if we stay out here a little longer.'

Her heart was thumping frantically fast. She didn't want to stay outside alone with him. She wanted to be with everyone else. Where she would be safe ... But safe from what? He wasn't threatening her in any way. He wasn't even touching her any more, and dangerously, in view of all she knew about him, her skin actually seemed to miss that cool contact with his fingers.

'You rather intrigue me, you know,' he told her, moving round so that he was facing her.

'Oh. Am I supposed to find that flattering?'

'Don't you?'

Reaction kicked at her stomach. He knew too much... Saw too much.

'No,' she told him shortly. 'And now, if you'll excuse me, I must go back.'

She side-stepped him, expelling a shaky breath of relief when he let her, and then just as she thought herself safe he reached out and circled her wrist, shackling her to him.

'Not yet,' he told her softly. 'You realise, don't you, that you're the reason I'm here today?'

'No.' She made the denial instinctively, choking over the word as he coolly drew her to him and into his arms.

Why was he doing this... and why was she letting him? She was a fool, an idiot, bent on self-destruction. She tried to escape but it was too late. His mouth was already hard and warm on hers. His hands were smoothing down over her back. In another moment her body would be pressed the whole length of his and he would be doing to her what he had done before.

Panic engulfed her. She didn't want this... She hadn't invited it. But she hadn't rejected it either, an inner voice taunted her. She struggled to pull herself away from him, to evade the drugging pressure of his mouth.

'Luke... Luke, where are you?'

Natasha gasped in relief as she heard Sara calling Luke's name.

'Luke, you promised me this dance.'

She thought she heard him curse under his breath as he released her, but her heart was pounding so heavily that she was surprised she could hear anything above its roar.

As she stepped away from him she saw that in the moonlight the flesh around his mouth was tight with anger. He hadn't wanted to let her go, she recognised, as Sara spotted them and came rushing over.

'Oh, there you are. This is our dance. Emma wants you,' she told Natasha dismissively. 'She says she's ready to get changed.'

Natasha was only too happy to escape.

'You look pale. Are you OK?' Emma asked her when they went upstairs to her room.

'Yes. I'm fine.'

'Fancy Luke turning up like that...and he's given us a very generous cheque.'

'And that makes everything all right?' Natasha asked her bitterly. 'Emma, less than a month ago you were convinced the man was going to destroy your whole life.'

'Well, that's what I thought... I still think he *might* have done if you hadn't pretended to be me. Has he said anything more about that to you?' she questioned anxiously.

'No,' Natasha told her abruptly.

Somewhere in the marquee Luke would be dancing with Sara. She told herself that she was glad that Richard's young sister had interrupted them, that the last thing she would have wanted was to be forced to endure the intimacy he had been pressing on her, and yet some tiny part of her body remained unconvinced, and the flesh of her mouth felt tender and sensitive so that when she touched it with her fingertips she could still almost feel the sensation of Luke's mouth there.

Three hours later, when the last of the wedding guests had gone, including Luke, Natasha felt more exhausted than she had ever done in her life. It wasn't just the wedding itself, it was the strain of avoiding Luke—of avoiding confronting the duality of her responses to him.

On the surface were her natural resentment, her ire, her fury, and yet beneath them ran a dangerous flow of counter emotions. Arousal, desire, sexual excitement. Emotions as unfamiliar to her as they were unwanted.

Emotions she must get firmly under control because they had no place in her life. No place at all. Neither had Luke Templecombe.

# CHAPTER FIVE

WHY was it, Natasha wondered grimly three weeks after the wedding, that the phone always chose to ring with the particularly irritatingly imperious summons when she was either halfway up or halfway down her small four-storey home's flights of stairs, and therefore forced to race either up or down them to silence its aggravating demands.

Another person—an Emma no doubt—would probably have cheerfully allowed it to ring. Or have an additional phone socket installed on the first-storey landing, she decided breathlessly as she reached the door of her workroom and flung it open, dashing across the room to snatch up the receiver, saying quickly, 'Natasha Lacey.'

There was a small silence of a kind that made a tiny thrill of premonition race down her spine, and then a faintly mocking male voice drawled, 'And a rather out of breath Natasha Lacey at that. Very flattering, I must say.'

The voice, the lazy amusement, the sexual self-confidence were all of them instantly recognisable, as was the sharp thrill of betraying sensation that burned through her. But after them came panic and then fear. Why was Luke Templecombe tele-phoning her? Just for a moment she was tempted to pretend that she hadn't recognised his voice, or, even better, that she didn't remember him at all, but caution warned her that to do so would be to enter into a very dangerous game indeed. One at which she suspected he was adept and skilled, and one for which she already knew she had no talents at all, so instead she said as coolly as she could, 'Luke—what an unexpected surprise. If you've been trying to get in touch with Richard's parents, I believe they've gone away for a few days.'

He didn't take up the polite fiction she was offering, saying after a small pause, 'No, it was you I wanted to talk to. I have some business in the city next week. I'll be staying over for a couple of days. Richard's parents are very kindly allowing me to use the deanery as a *pied-à-terre*. I'll be there for three days. I'd like to take you out to dinner.'

To say she was stunned was a massive understatement, Natasha thought muzzily as she stared silently out the window. She had never expected Luke to get in touch with her again, and never, ever, in her wildest imaginings visualised him calmly inviting her out. Her workroom had been warmed by the sun all day, and initially when she had rushed in she had found it almost overpoweringly hot. Now suddenly she shivered, rashes of goose-flesh breaking out over her skin.

She had tried so hard to dismiss that sharp, fierce sexual arousal she had experienced in Luke's arms, to pretend that helpless spiralling sensation of her body bursting to life beneath his hands and mouth had never happened, to obliterate from her memory the dangerous knowledge that Luke had been physically aroused by her, had wanted her, telling herself that she was a fool if she imagined that he was doing anything other than deliberately and consciously using his maleness in that way to punish her, knowing almost just by looking at him that his experience of life, of human emotions and vulnerabilities was light years away from her own, reminding herself that his particular brand of maleness was both potent and dangerous, particularly to someone like her, who did not have the experience to combat it.

Had they met in different circumstances, had she not unwisely allowed Emma to persuade her to adopt a persona that was not really hers, had he been introduced to her as she really was, Natasha suspected that Luke would have treated her with the same good-mannered but distancing politeness she had witnessed him exhibiting to such good effect on Richard's mother. It was partly her own fault that he had reacted to her in the sexually predatory manner he had, and it had stunned her to discover how naïve, how defenceless, how very unaware of her own vulnerability she had been.

She had never believed it was possible to react so immediately and so intensely to a man one didn't very much like. It had shocked her to discover within herself a hitherto hidden streak of recklessness so contradictory to her normal carefully controlled behaviour. A recklessness which whispered provocatively that perhaps it was time she had the experience of a Luke Templecombe in her life. So had spoken the serpent to Eve!

Now Luke was ringing her up, asking her out, and she was not so naïve that she didn't realise that it wasn't her conversation he wanted. This kind of experience, this casual, emotionless assumption that she would welcome what she knew would only be a brief sexual fling with him chilled her, bringing home to her her own danger.

She took a deep breath and, before she could give in to the temptation churning recklessly inside her, said shakily, 'I'm sorry... That won't be possible.'

The silence from the other end of the line was almost menacing. He obviously wasn't used to being turned down, she told herself, trying to whip up enough anger to subdue the dangerous *frisson* of yearning twisting inside her. If she accepted and went out with him, it would lead to all manner of complications. He thought she was one of his own kind, and when he discovered she wasn't it would lead to embarrassment and maybe even pain. The mere fact that she was tempted to accept warned her how dangerously vulnerable she was. It was pointless allowing herself to ignore the facts, to indulge in silly, impossible daydreams.

For her own sake, she had to make sure that he did not get in touch with her again.

'So you're not free next week,' the silky voice enquired.

She took a deep breath, knowing what she had to say.

'I'm sorry, but I'm not free at all.'

'I see.'

How odd that two words said in such an expressionless manner could convey such a wealth of ironic innuendo.

Later she acknowledged painfully that she ought to have left it there, simply said goodbye and replaced the receiver, but the same impulse that had made her feel guilty and responsible enough to help Emma out of so many ridiculous situations now pushed her to add, 'In fact, I can't imagine why you should think that I might want to see you again.'

There was a small silence and she thought for a moment that she had gained ascendancy over him, and then as smooth as cream and far, far less palatable came the words, 'Really? I have memories of a certain handful of minutes which tell a very different story. However, I can quite well understand why in these health conscious times you might not want to be seen as a woman who shares her bed with two lovers concurrently. You must forgive me. I must be becoming rather less astute than I have always believed myself to be. I didn't realise that you were already involved elsewhere...'

It was just as well she was alone, Natasha reflected as she felt the indignant anger scald a hot, burning tide across her body. How dared he insinuate... Her fingers tightened around the receiver. She ached to let him know just how wrong he was, to give voice to her fury and resentment that he should dare to criticise *her* behaviour, to imply that it was her fault that he had assumed that she was both available and willing to play sophisticated sexual games with him. But she couldn't do so without betraying Emma.

Even so, she was angry enough to say icily, 'Even if I weren't, I assure you that I would have no interest whatsoever in pursuing our acquaintance.'

With that she slammed down the receiver, but not before she had heard him saying cynically, 'Odd . . . that wasn't the message I received at all.'

Hateful, hateful man! How dared he assume. . .? how dared he suggest . . .?

She was still pacing her workroom half an hour later when the phone rang a second time. She looked at it doubtfully, half inclined to let it ring, and then, telling herself that she was being stupid, she made herself pick up the receiver.

The sensation she experienced when she discovered that her caller wasn't Luke Templecombe wasn't entirely one of relief. Which told its own betraying and dangerous story, she reflected grimly as she tried to concentrate on her telephone call.

It was rather a long one, and when it was over she found herself torn between relief and a rather disturbing sense of disappointment. What she ought to be feeling was elation, she chastised herself. It wasn't every day that she received such a prestigious commission.

An invitation to select and quote for fabrics to complement the renovation of a Carolean manor house which was presently being converted into an exclusive private hotel wasn't the kind of commission that someone in her position could afford to be blasé about. What was even more heart-warming was that the owner of the hotel had seen some fabrics she had supplied for someone else and had liked them so much that he had immediately found out her name and got in touch with her. He was anxious to keep the flavour and period. of the house as authentic as possible, he had told her, bearing in mind the fact that, being in a hotel, the fabrics would be subject to the kind of wear and tear not recommended for rare antiques.

He had suggested that she spend a week at the house as his guest so that she would have plenty of time to absorb its atmosphere and consider what fabrics would best complement it. Although she had pointed out to him that she was no interior designer, he did not seem to think this a problem, telling her briskly that he would much prefer to have the opinion and suggestions of someone with a genuine feel and flare for the period rather than a designer intent on meeting some fashionable criteria without proper thought for the ambiance he wanted to give the place.

It was the kind of challenge she had often day-dreamed about, but never imagined actually being given, Natasha acknowledged. If she had received this kind of offer before meeting Luke Templecombe it would have filled her every waking thought, but now her gratification was tinged with an odd reluctance to accept a commission which she knew would take her out of the city when Luke was due to visit it. Why, when she already knew that the worst thing she could do was to fall into the trap of letting herself believe that by some miracle Luke was going to take one look at her, realise how badly he had misjudged her and immediately announce how much he preferred the real Natasha?

Not only was she a fool for imagining anything so impossible could actually happen, she was also dangerously close to the border of some kind of

emotional suicide if she actually *wanted* Luke to...
To what? To desire her? To pursue her? To what
end? The kind of involvement she had determinedly avoided all her adult life—the kind of
involvement that was based on emotionless sexual
need on the man's part, and something frighteningly close to total emotional and permanent commitment on the woman's?

She had always known that within herself lay this
deep pool of emotional vulnerability, this capacity
to give herself completely and absolutely to one man
and one alone. What she had never known was how
easily the man in question could be someone like
Luke Templecombe, the kind of man who was, of
all his sex, least likely to either want or be able to
share the intensity of her emotional commitment.

It was just as well that only she knew of that
momentary surge of reluctance to accept the
commission she had been offered. Telling herself
that what she was experiencing was probably
nothing more than a good old-fashioned and
probably overdue dose of totally unsuitable sexual
responsiveness, she resolved to put Luke
Templecombe right out of her mind.

Three days later, irritated with herself for her
inability to close off her mind against its insidious
clinging to her memories of Luke, Natasha was
walking in Lacey Court's gardens, trying to clear
the persistent headache which she knew was born
of a combination of lack of sleep and mental unrest.

What increased her self-anger was the knowledge
that, instead of wasting time spending so much
energy and emotion dwelling on a man who ought

to have no place in any sane woman's thoughts, she should have been concentrating on preparing herself for what was the most important commission she had ever received.

A year ago, a month ago even, had someone told her that she would have actually been in this kind of emotional state, where she preferred day-dreaming impossible daydreams about a man whose every word and gesture was completely opposed to everything she believed went to make up the type of man who most appealed to her to concentrating her every thought and effort on the most exciting challenge of her new career, she would have dismissed them as insane.

Now *she* was the one who was dangerously close to insanity. She had to be, to be virtually yearning as helplessly as a teenager over a man whom every protective instinct she possessed told her it was imperative she kept out of her life.

The trouble was that she had other instincts—deeper, more dangerous, and innately stronger instincts, instincts she had never dreamed existed until Luke had so shockingly awakened them; instincts which recklessly told her that, no matter what the risks, the dangers, she *must* allow her body the self-indulgence of experiencing all the pleasures it knew Luke Templecombe could show it.

As a child, Natasha had often stood on a bridge, looking down at the water flowing below, and experienced the dangerous sensation of being pulled towards that flow. Now she was experiencing that sensation again, only this time it was Luke Templecombe who was the magnet which drew her so dangerously, or rather the sexual spark he seemed to have ignited inside her.

She stopped her pacing, grimacing in self-disgust that she, who had always been so fiercely fastidious, so intensely protective of her own physical privacy, should experience this overwhelming surge of sexual hunger—the kind of hunger she had never associated with women like herself, the kind of hunger that kept her awake at night and made her body ache in a thousand unfamiliar and tormenting ways, that caused her, when she did sleep, to wake up from dreams of such intensity and sensuality that merely to remember odd flashes of them was enough to make her skin burn and her mind flinch.

'Dear me, surely it isn't my poor delphiniums that are causing that glower. I know this pink variety is somewhat frowned on by the purists, but they do add a certain balance to this section of the border.'

Natasha forced a smile as she saw her aunt approaching her, but it didn't come easily—something which the other woman obviously recognised, because as she stood beside her she asked quietly, 'Is something wrong, Tasha? This commission perhaps . . . I know it's a wonderful opportunity, but——'

'It isn't the commission,' Natasha assured her, and then realised what her denial had admitted.

'There is something, then?' Helen queried, confirming her thoughts.

For a moment Natasha was tempted to fib. She was a woman, not a child. This was the kind of problem she ought to be able to solve by herself; talking about it would do nothing other than to confirm what she already knew—that she had made the right decision in making it plain to Luke Templecombe that she did not want to pursue any kind of relationship with him. However, she had admitted too much to lie now; she was not blessed with the kind of inventive tongue which allowed her to fabricate deceit, and so she said quietly, 'It's nothing really. It's just that I got myself into a rather silly situation with someone and——'

'By someone I imagine you must mean Luke Templecombe,' her aunt interrupted her, concealing her own compassion when she saw the way Natasha looked at her. This niece of hers was so vulnerable, so different from her own ebullient, lightweight daughter.

Shocked, Natasha rushed into unguarded speech. 'How did you know? I mean...'

'I saw him follow you out into the garden, the evening of Emma's pre-wedding dinner.'

Despairingly, Natasha closed her eyes and then opened them again, suddenly longing to unburden herself.

'Let's go and sit down,' her aunt suggested, leading the way to a sheltered stone bench situated to give the best view of the high summer border.

Humbly Natasha followed her. As soon as they were seated, she found herself pouring out everything in a disjointed, confused spate of words, so unlike her normal concise, often guarded conversation that Helen Lacey felt her concern increase.

Listening to Natasha's breathless speech, she found time to mentally chastise Emma's part in the confusion, thinking it typical of her flighty child that she should involve her more serious cousin in what by rights should have been her own problems, with scant regard for the possible consequences to Natasha.

'So perhaps because of the way you were dressed, and certainly because you had stepped so protectively into Emma's shoes, Luke mistook you for——'

'For Jake Pendraggon's lover,' Natasha agreed, adding quickly, 'Not of course that Emma and Jake were lovers. I suspect she simply wanted to make Richard jealous.'

'Well, she certainly succeeded, and to such effect that when it became necessary she could not rely on his believing the truth. She behaved very badly— very badly, involving you in what should have been her own problem. I suppose it wouldn't be possible to tell Luke the truth?' Helen hazarded, suspecting that there was more to the story than she was being told.

Her cautious, defensive niece would not normally be sent into such a state by the unwelcome advances of a sexually predatory male, so what was different about this one? She suspected she already knew, and her heart ached for Natasha.

'I *can't* tell him the truth...' And not just because of Emma. Her own pride would not allow her to do so. And not just her pride. For some reason she didn't want to see the bored uninterest she already knew would creep into his eyes once he learned the truth about her—that she was a dull, undesired twenty-seven-year-old virgin, who had been entrapped into playing a role for which she was completely unsuited, and who was now so scared by the results of that role-playing that she was forced to admit the truth.

'Oh, dear,' was her aunt's only very mild comment.

As she looked at the older woman, Natasha knew quite well that her aunt had correctly interpreted the complexities of her emotions.

'I take it, then, that this new commission has arrived at a most fortuitous time?'

'Yes,' Natasha agreed shakily, glad that she didn't have to put into words her fears that if she stayed in the area she would be all too vulnerable to any pressure Luke decided to put her under. She said as much to her aunt.

'Mm,' the latter agreed, 'a very dangerous young man. I thought so the moment I set eyes on him, and I can't help wondering if it was entirely wise of you to suggest to him that you're involved with somebody else.'

'It was the only thing I could think of to put him off,' Natasha told her. 'It certainly seemed to work.'

She winced a little, remembering his acerbic, almost cruel comment.

'Perhaps,' her aunt agreed, 'although he struck me as a man who has no compunction whatsoever about meeting whatever challenges life chooses to throw his way. As you say, it's probably just as well that you're going to be out of his reach for the next few weeks. He is very compelling, Natasha, almost overpoweringly so, and very attractive.'

'So is fire,' Natasha retorted drily, 'providing you don't get too close to it.'

Her aunt gave her a shrewd, compassionate look. 'I see. Like that, was it?' She saw Natasha's expression and smiled reminiscently. 'I haven't entirely forgotten what it feels like, you know. Even when one gets to my age, one isn't automatically rendered unsusceptible to one's emotional and physical needs. Just look at that iris,' she directed, drawing Natasha's attention to the flower in question. 'Isn't it the most perfect colour?'

It was, and Natasha said as much, recognising that her aunt wished to turn their conversation away from any more personal confidences.

'This border always looks its best at this time of year,' her aunt continued, as they left their seat and started to walk towards the house, 'although this year I'm wondering about extending its life by underplanting the perennials with autumn flowering bulbs.'

They continued to discuss the garden until they had returned to the back door, where her aunt left Natasha, announcing that she had to go and check on the progress of her sweet peas.

For the rest of the time left before she was due to leave for Stonelovel Manor, Natasha stalwartly refused to allow her thoughts any leniency to wander in the direction of Luke Templecombe. It wasn't easy; temptation had a way of presenting itself to her in so many plausible guises that sometimes even she herself was deceived.

The fact that this, her most challenging and potentially most demanding commission to date, made it necessary for her to involve herself in a certain amount of preparatory research before leaving Sutton Minster helped.

Her knowledge garnered during her recent investigative trips to Florence in particular had already equipped her with an excellent store of knowledge to draw on, and even more a supply of contacts in that city whom she hoped would be able to supply the various decorative items she wanted to suggest to Leo Rosenberg as ideal to complement the rich damasks and tapestries she wanted to use.

In Florence there were frame-makers, adept at copying any frame a client chose to desire, small, old-fashioned workshops tucked away in narrow down-at-heel streets where every kind of panelling, moulding or other decorative item of work could be produced as skilfully today as it had been centuries before. These craftsmen were expensive, of course, but she had gained the impression from Leo Rosenberg that this venture represented something that was more than a mere commercial venture.

On her father's advice, she had made some discreet cautionary enquiries via her bank, for as her father had warned her, for someone like herself, newly established in her own business, the financial hardship of buying for a client who then turned out not to be in a position to pay for goods ordered on his behalf could destroy her business and leave her with a burden of debts she could never repay.

The bank reports were good, and some further enquiries made by her solicitors elicited the information that Leo Rosenberg was a man in his early fifties who by judicious buying and selling of property had built up a reputation as a shrewd entrepreneur.

His decision to buy Stonelovel Manor and convert it, not into expensive and sought after apartments, but instead into a luxury country house hotel had caused some surprise in financial circles, but the general force of opinion seemed to be that Leo Rosenberg had the Midas touch when it came to his business affairs.

Having reassured himself that his daughter was not going to be drawn into financial over-trading, Natasha's father offered to give her whatever help she might need in completing the commission.

'I've got to get it first,' Natasha reminded him, the night before she was due to leave for Stonelovel. She was poring over maps at the time, checking up on the best route from her home to the manor, having decided not to use the direct route of the M4, and then to cut across country, but instead to take her time and enjoy a quieter if more circuitous route that meandered through the countryside.

Only she knew that she had deliberately decided to leave a full day before she had originally planned, because suddenly in the middle of the night she had woken up from a dream in which Luke Templecombe had presented himself at her front door a day before he was due to arrive. Wishful thinking or presentiment? What did it matter? What did matter was the aching, yearning burden of temptation the dream brought her, the almost uncontrollable desire to simply give in and let fate carry her where it willed.

But allowing someone or something else to take over her life, to make her decision for her, and thus to abdicate from the responsibility of any decision about it, was not and never had been Natasha's way, so she sturdily fought down the wakening, desirous wash of dangerous allure trying to erode her self-will, and decided to leave a day early.

A quick check by telephone to the number Leo Rosenberg had given her confirmed that it would be in order for her to do this.

'Leo is at present abroad,' his secretary informed her, but a room had been organised for her at the house, and his staff had been primed to expect her. 'The place is full of workmen at the moment, but Leo should be back tomorrow. You'll want to have a good look round the house, of course, and that's why Leo thought it would be a good idea for you to stay there for a few days, to get the feel of the house; and I know he wants to talk to you about his own ideas and plans for the ambiance he wants to create.'

Now, knowing that she wanted to get an early start in the morning, Natasha checked through the samples of fabric she had put on one side to take with her, and then went meticulously through the portfolio of photographs she had culled from various magazines, the brochures she had obtained from various manufacturers of reproduction furniture, and all the other details she had meticulously gathered together, including her all-important notebooks from her trip to Florence.

This was the most important challenge of her career, and she was not going to allow anything or anyone to deflect her from giving it her full attention—especially not Luke Templecombe.

'I'll be leaving early in the morning,' she told her parents as she stood up, 'so I'll say goodbye now and I'll try not to disturb you in the morning.'

'You'll ring us when you arrive, won't you?' her mother queried anxiously. 'The roads these days——'

'I'll ring you just as soon as I can,' Natasha soothed.

She knew that she was taking the only sensible course open to her, that in this instance flight was definitely safer than fight, but her pride chafed at the necessity of it, wishing that she had the courage, the armour to confront Luke.

But it wasn't confronting him she feared; it wasn't that at all... What she feared was the enemy within herself, the alien, invidious physical desire he seemed to stir up inside her with so little effort. *That* was why she was running away. Had she not felt that desire, had he simply been another unwanted male importuning her, she would have had no compunction at all about staying and making it plain to him that he was wasting his time, but she doubted her own ability to tell him she didn't want him when her body had so plainly and shockingly already given her a very different message indeed.

And yet why was she allowing herself to get into such a state? Almost the first thing that had struck her about Luke was his male pride, so sharp-edged and honed that it almost bordered on arrogance. *Why* was she so afraid he would attempt to pursue her when she had told him she was involved with someone else?

Though he was no saint sexually himself, she had known instinctively that he was a man who would not share—a man who would never tolerate his current lover's being involved with another man. She had said enough to him surely to ensure that he must have lost whatever interest he had had in her, and yet beneath that logical certainty ran another kind of knowledge, a thread of instinct and deep feminine awareness that warned that, no matter what she might have told him vocally, her body had given him other, subtler, but no less emotive messages which he might just choose to believe in preference to her spoken words.

He was above everything else a man of intense pride, and who could tell? He might just choose to take it into his head to force her to acknowledge that, no matter how much she might say she did not want him, that she was involved with someone else, physically she desired *him*. And if once he did that . . .

She shivered suddenly, goose-bumps a rash of intense sensation along her skin as her body treacherously remembered how it had felt to be in his arms.

Stop it, she told herself. Stop it now before it's too late.

Thank goodness she had been offered this commission so opportunely. Without it, without the necessity of taking herself away from him, she doubted that she would have found the strength to do so voluntarily.

# CHAPTER SIX

'DO COME in. Suzie, Leo's PA, rang and warned us to expect you. Aren't we being lucky with the weather at the moment?'

Acknowledging the older woman's pleasantries, Natasha followed Leo Rosenberg's housekeeper into the house.

She had arrived five minutes earlier, knocked on the door and introduced herself, and as the older woman invited her inside Natasha paused to study her surroundings.

'Leo intends to keep the reception-rooms as much as possible as they already are. Upstairs, of course, there's a great deal of work to be done; rooms have to be divided, bathrooms et cetera, but then of course you'll know all about that.'

Before Natasha could confirm or deny her comments, the housekeeper was leading her through the hall, opening a door set in the rear wall.

'We've tried to give you a room where you won't be disturbed too much by the workmen, but as you can see everything's rather chaotic at the moment,' she apologised, raising her voice so that Natasha could hear her above the sound of men whistling, electric drills whirring and the general hubbub of people working.

'We're all sleeping on the top floor at the moment, and I'm afraid we're having to use what used to be the servants' staircase, which is rather narrow; Leo intends to have lifts installed, discreetly of course.'

The stairs were narrow, and very twisty in places, but Natasha, used to the vagaries of her parents' home and her own steep four-storey little house, was far less breathless when they reached the top than her guide.

'Your room's down here,' the housekeeper told her. 'No private bathroom, I'm afraid, although you won't actually have to share with anyone else. Leo's organised a suite for himself at the other end of the house, in what will eventually be his private wing. My room is at the top of the staircase, and at the moment no one else is actually staying here.' She paused outside a white-painted door, and opened it.

Stepping inside, Natasha saw that she had been given a room with a big window which faced north, and which would be ideal for her to work in. It was a good-sized room, equipped with a double bed, a couple of comfortable looking armchairs, a desk, an easel and even an open fire.

'Leo said that you'd need somewhere where you'd be able to work in private as well as sleep. This was the room the architect used when he was drawing up the original plans for the alterations. I hope it will be all right.'

'It's ideal,' Natasha assured her, giving the woman the warm smile which always transformed her face, banishing the faintly aloof elegance which it had in repose, and drawing the immediate response of a relieved smile from the other woman.

'Well, that's all right, then. I'm afraid I've rather been dreading your arrival. I wasn't sure if Leo had warned you what to expect. He tends to talk about the house as though it's already been transformed, forgetting to warn people about the realities of the work in progress.'

'You've known him a long time?' Natasha hazarded.

'Yes. My husband used to work for him when he first set up in business, then, when George was killed in a road accident, Leo asked me if I'd like to come and work for him. It was a real lifeline. George and I had no children, no family at all to speak of... That was fifteen years ago and I've been with Leo ever since. He even offered to send me on a special course, so that I could run the hotel as its housekeeper once all the work is finished, but it would be too much responsibility for me and I told him so.'

So the ruthless, efficient entrepreneur of her father's business reports had a human side, Natasha reflected as she listened. Certainly his enthusiasm and love for the house had suggested that he was far from being the typical hard-headed type such men were generally assumed to be.

'I'll leave you to get settled in, then. Leo is coming down tomorrow to go round the place with you.'

Natasha had been hoping to explore the house on her own before meeting her client, but, having seen the extent of the work in progress on the fabric of the building, was forced to admit that it might be wiser to wait until Leo Rosenberg arrived in case she got in the way of the workmen.

'Would it be all right if I explored the gardens?' she asked the housekeeper now. 'I don't want to get in anyone's way.'

'They haven't started work on those as yet, so I should think that will be all right. Leo did say that if you were interested there were some books and papers in his study describing various changes which have been made to the place over the years.'

'I'd love to see them,' Natasha agreed.

An hour later, wandering around the neglected kitchen garden, reflecting on how much her aunt would enjoy the challenge of restoring it to what it must have once been, the guard she had placed on herself slipped, and without even knowing how it had happened she found herself thinking about another garden...another time...about a certain evening and a certain man. Before she knew what she was doing, in her mind's eye she saw Luke walking towards her front door, ringing the bell, waiting impatiently, and then, when there was no response, walking away. As she watched that departing back, she had an insane impulse to run to her car, to drive home just as fast as she could so that... So that what? So that she could open her heart and her mind to the inevitable pain which would follow any involvement with a man like Luke? What was the matter with her? She had never thought of herself as being a masochistic type before. Quite the contrary.

It had been a lovely day, and here in the enclosed kitchen garden it was almost hot, and yet still she shivered visibly, a violent tremor of sensation running through her body. Why was she reacting like this, feeling like this, aching, yearning, hungering like this, when she knew that the man responsible for these unwanted, dangerous feelings could offer her nothing other than an emotionally barren physical affair?

She stopped in front of what had once been a bed of herbs, and bent automatically to remove a large chickweed while her thoughts went round and round in the same tormenting circles.

'It's a disgrace, isn't it? I saw you walking from my study window and I thought I'd better come down and introduce myself.'

Natasha straightened up, flushing a little as she saw the amused and faintly speculative eyes of the man who had approached her.

Tall, somewhere in his early fifties, still dark-haired with a penetrating, thoughtful gaze, he made her all too conscious that the appearance she must be presenting was hardly the one she would have wished to present.

'Leo Rosenberg,' he introduced himself, shaking her hand firmly, ignoring the particles of soil clinging to her, and giving her a genuinely warm smile as he asked, 'Do you know much about gardening? I confess I'm at a loss to know where to begin with this one. What I'd like is to restore it as far as possible to something approaching a style in keeping with the house, although, bearing in mind that this is going to be a hotel, allowances will have

to be made for the inclusion of tennis-courts et
cetera.'

'I'm not an expert on gardens, I'm afraid,'
Natasha confessed, 'but my aunt is, and I know
she'd love to get her teeth into something like this,
starting virtually from scratch——' She broke off,
flushing again. 'I'm sorry. It's just that I was
thinking about her . . . about how much she'd enjoy
the challenge of this garden.'

'She needs a challenge, does she?' he asked
astutely, causing Natasha to reflect that she was
already beginning to see just what made this man
so financially successful.

'I think so, although she'd probably disagree with
me,' Natasha admitted as she fell into step beside
him. She hadn't introduced herself, but it was
obvious that he knew who she was.

'Knows a bit about this kind of thing, does she?'
he enquired, making a sweeping gesture towards the
area they were just leaving.

'An awful lot,' Natasha agreed. 'It's her hobby,
and the gardens at home are her special province.
I hadn't realised you were arriving this afternoon,'
she continued a little more formally. She didn't want
him to think she had been taking advantage of his
absence to simply waste time. 'Your housekeeper
told me you were arriving tomorrow to go over the
house with me. I didn't want to disturb the
workmen.'

'No, best not to,' he agreed, explaining, 'I
managed to get away earlier than I expected. There's
something wonderfully relaxing about coming back
to this place.'

He stopped and breathed in deeply. Despite his age and occupation he looked remarkably fit, Natasha noticed, the involuntary movement of his chest as he breathed in betraying a solid muscle structure, devoid of excess flesh. Her thoughts were confirmed when he removed his jacket and slung it over his shoulder.

'Yes, I must admit I don't envy you working in London,' Natasha admitted.

The grin he gave her was endearingly boyish.

'Not London on this occasion. I've just flown in from New York and, as you say, here is infinitely preferable. That's why I intend to retire—to retain one wing of the house for my own private use, and live what's left of my life at a more relaxed pace.

'Unfortunately, in order to do that, initially I'm having to put in a lot of extra time getting every-thing sorted out. This aunt of yours—where can I find her?'

His question startled Natasha into an automatic reply, and she was even more startled when he frowned and then said thoughtfully, 'Laceys...of course...Ecclesiastical Textiles. I ought to have realised. You've virtually grown up in the business, then?'

'Yes, although I did break away from it for a while.'

Funny how easy it was to talk to this man, Natasha reflected. He had that same gift of genuine interest in others which she so admired in her aunt.

Thinking of Helen made her wonder a little guiltily how the latter would react if Leo Rosenberg did call on her. Perhaps she ought to warn her—

but then she had no idea if her new client was simply making conversation or whether he was seriously considering asking her aunt to help him with the restoration of his garden.

'I'm sorry if I'm pushing you a bit, but I've got an unexpected meeting in Amsterdam tomorrow, and if we could go round the house together now, and then go over the architect's plans . . .'

'I'd love to,' Natasha assured him. 'I've been doing as much reading up on the period as I can, and I've brought some samples with me, plus some sketches. As far as the bedrooms go, obviously you're going to want them to work from a practical point of view, as well as echo a feel for the period. Where the reception-rooms are concerned, I'm not sure just how much authenticity you had in mind. Obviously again the rooms are going to be used.'

'Used, yes, but we expect that the kind of guests we attract will have a genuine interest in and respect for antiques. Naturally, I'm not suggesting we re-create a Carolean interior exact in every detail—that would be impossible—but to some extent, encouraging the guests to believe that they have stepped back into the past, that they are staying somewhere which genuinely reflects a feeling for the period in which it was first built. I'm not suggesting using original antique fabrics, even if they could be found—such things more properly belong in museums and collections—but new fabrics, copied from original designs, made in the traditional way.'

Several hours later, when Leo Rosenberg had shown her the length and breadth of the house,

Natasha found herself liking him even more than she had done at first.

Wisely she had allowed him to lead the conversation. She always found it easier to help a client once she had discovered exactly how they felt about their home and its role in their lives, and, despite the fact that primarily Leo had called her in to provide interior design for the hotel, she had quickly discovered that the house meant far more to him than merely another business venture.

'There's nothing I'd like more than to simply keep the place as a private home,' he confided when they were back in the small cluttered room he was using as a temporary office. 'But, as the last owner discovered, it takes enormous revenues to maintain a place like this as a private house. I simply could not afford to do it. Sooner or later I'd have to sell and watch it being split up into separate units, its ambiance lost . . .

'I called in a team of consultants, got them to advise me on the best way to make a place like this pay its own way. They came up with the idea of converting it into a select country house hotel—the kind that caters for a maximum of ten couples and is more like joining a private house party than staying at a hotel. The American and Japanese in particular love that sort of thing. As you know, Charlie, the chef, is Roux-brothers trained. What I need to find now is a first-class hostess-cum-house-keeper——'

He broke off, grinning slightly shamefacedly. 'I'm sorry, but I'm afraid I do tend to get carried away once I start, and you're a very sympathetic listener.'

'Won't your wife——?' Natasha began, but he shook his head, cutting her off.

'I'm a widower. My wife died five years ago. She'd been ill for a long time. She developed a progressive wasting disease after the birth of our son.'

Natasha made a soft sound of sympathy, and then, sensing that it wasn't a subject he wanted to pursue, said quietly, 'I've got a rather interesting article upstairs which you might like to read. I came across it by chance, but it's very informative. It's about the resurgence of interest in traditionally patterned and made fabrics, and I think you'll find the section on damasks and brocades of particular interest. As you may know, my father's factory mainly produces ecclesiastical cloths, although he is extending his range to include several non-ecclesiastical traditional designs. However, there are factories in Italy mainly, in and around Florence, where they still have the original pattern books which they have used for centuries, where they can still produce what is virtually, in everything but age, an original seventeenth-century cloth.

'It's expensive, of course,' she warned, 'and I would suggest only for use in certain carefully selected places.'

By the end of the evening, Natasha had discovered that her latest client was not a man who believed in wasting time once he had made up his mind about something. Subject to his final approval, he had virtually given her *carte blanche* to go ahead with designing and furnishing, not only the bedrooms for the new hotel, but the reception-rooms as well, and with a budget which made her gape a little at him.

'The kind of guest I want to attract will expect it,' he told her, but it seemed to Natasha that he was being a little defensive and she warmed to him even more, sensing his desire to clothe the house in the very best raiment he could afford out of love for it, rather than out of a far more businesslike desire to win the approval of potential guests.

As she had discovered, when it came to the small wing of the house which he was retaining for his private use he had very definite ideas about what he wanted, but he had obviously done his homework, and where fabrics were concerned he had made it plain to Natasha that he was perfectly happy to be guided by her.

'I have a small collection of paintings which I intend to hang in the long gallery of my own wing. A friend of mine is going to advise me as to their placement. I've been scouring the auction houses and dealers for suitable pieces of furniture for my own wing. As far as the hotel is concerned, most of the furniture will have to be reproduction and purpose-built, in a style in keeping with the period, of course.'

It was after one in the morning before Natasha was finally able to go upstairs to bed. He would be leaving for Amsterdam first thing in the morning, Leo Rosenberg had told her, but she was to stay on as originally arranged until his return, when hopefully they would be able to finalise the initial colour schemes for the individual guest bedrooms.

As they said their goodnights, it occurred to Natasha that at heart Leo Rosenberg was a lonely man, even though on the surface he seemed to have everything in life that a human being could want, and her own heart felt chilled and heavy as she prepared for bed and contemplated her own future. A lonely future. A future without love, without passion…without Luke, who, she reminded herself hardily, was hardly likely to furnish her with either love or passion, but merely with the base coin of physical desire. Was she really stupid enough to believe that she could ever be happy with that kind of relationship? Of course not!

So why was she wasting so much time, so many thoughts, so much heartache in thinking about him, in wanting him? *Wanting* him? She sat up in bed and shuddered. *Why* did she want him? Why was she behaving in a way that for her was so out of character? She already knew that Luke had nothing genuine to offer her, nothing that for her could make the dangers of their relationship worthwhile.

With this new commission to fill her thoughts and her time, it ought to have been the easiest thing in the world to put him out of her thoughts. Instead…instead, here she was lying sleepless in a strange bed, knowing that if she closed her eyes, if she allowed herself to relax, she would end up as she had ended up on so many nights recently, reliving every touch, every word, every heartbeat of the time she had already spent with him, and that, worse, within seconds of admitting his memory into her thoughts she would be aching for more than mere memories, that she would be... She made a soft sound of distress in her throat and turned over, thumping her pillow, telling herself that she was her own worst enemy, that she had to forget him, to put him right out of her mind, and concentrate not on fictional fantasy but on reality.

## CHAPTER SEVEN

IT WAS three days before Natasha saw Leo Rosenberg again, three days during which she worked extremely hard, both on preparing detailed drawings for each of the guest bedrooms and the reception-rooms, and on mentally closing the doors of her mind against the all too intrusive thoughts of Luke Templecombe which continued to plague her.

Of the two, preparing the drawings was by far the easier. She would go to bed at night, convinced that she was so exhausted both mentally and physically that she would be asleep the moment her head touched the pillow, only to find that she was wrong and that her aching, yearning body recalcitrantly refused to allow her the peace she needed.

On the third night before Leo's return, exhausted by a struggle which seemed to grow harder with time, rather than easier, she gave in and allowed her thoughts to conjure up impossible fantasies in which Luke suddenly appeared to sweep her off her feet, to hold her and kiss her as he had done on that never-to-be-forgotten night, but this time without anger, without cynicism, without the divisive resentment of her sex which had come across to her so clearly on that occasion.

All human beings had their own private defence systems, and, given the history of Luke's childhood, it wasn't impossible to understand that the fact that his mother had left both him and his father for another man, plus the tragedy of his father's eventual suicide, could have resulted in a resentment and mistrust of the female sex which had manifested itself in his relentless sexual pursuit of her.

She was no psychologist; she didn't need to be, she admitted, to recognise that she was looking for excuses, for explanations to offset the apparent deliberate emotionlessness of Luke's sexual overtures.

Moving restlessly in the comfortable bed, she lectured herself against the folly of believing that it was possible for Luke to change. Why should he? He obviously didn't want to. He was obviously quite happy with his way of life. She might not be sexually experienced, but it had been easy to see that Luke wanted only an emotionless sexual relationship with her.

Relationship. She smiled painfully to herself in the darkness. What made her think he wanted to take it that far? If she was brutally honest with herself, she had no reason to believe that Luke wanted anything more than simply to take her to bed, and then, once having done so, to forget her.

Why did that hurt so much? Her first instinct of dislike for him, her first rational awareness that he was cold and dangerous—they had been right. Just because later he had made her sexually aware of him, and just because her rebellious body for some unknown reasons of its own refused to forget or ignore that awareness, that did not mean she had to start looking for reasons, for excuses, for hope...

She shivered a little. It was her own upbringing, her own moral code that made her search for that leavening hint of emotion, of feeling, because she found it so difficult to accept that she could actually want a man who embodied everything she had always disliked in the male sex.

It had caught her off guard, shocked her, frightened her, that she could so easily be put into this state of emotional and physical turmoil, that she should have fled her home rather than confront him, that she should be lying here awake, thinking about him, wishing...

Wishing that what? That, like some romance-story hero, he would simply not take no for an answer, that he would overpower her veto with the strength of his determination and desire and thus remove from her the burden of decision, effectively consenting to a relationship which held nothing, none of those virtues she had always believed a man-to-woman relationship should hold?

The very thought revolted her. She had always prided herself on making her own decisions, on refusing to allow others to take any responsibility for them. If she ever allowed this physical attraction between them to develop, it would be because *she* had made a decision to do so, not because she had closed her eyes and simply allowed Luke to drag her into it so that she could then turn round and blame him.

*If* she ever allowed...her stomach turned over at the enormity of what she was thinking. What was happening to her? She had come here thinking that simply to remove herself from Luke's presence would be enough to cure her of this ridiculous desire she seemed to be suffering. She had genuinely believed that, kept mentally on her toes by her new commission, there would be no space in her mind for any thoughts of Luke . . .

How wrong she had been. Exhausted mentally and physically though she was, deep inside her body was a hunger, an ache which she knew would later cause her acute emotional and moral anguish, but which now was so sharp, so searing that she knew that if Luke were to open the door and walk into her room that ache would be a scream of physical need she might find it impossible to deny.

But why? Why now? Why this man? Why this intensity? It shocked her that her body could turn traitor on her like this, that she could want like this, ache like this, and above all it shocked her that she could experience this intensity without the saving grace of love.

She woke up tired, with dark circles round her eyes, knowing that today was the day she would have to present her suggestions and recommendations for Leo's approval.

Wearily she got up, and subjected herself to the hopefully energy-stimulating shock of a cold shower, shivering as the cold water burned goose-bumps into her shrinking flesh, forcing herself to endure the small punishment, knowing from experience she would feel the benefit of it later.

Her body wasn't something she was used to dwelling on overmuch. She was lucky in that she didn't tend to put on weight, and if privately she considered that she was a little on the slim side when compared to other women's rounded curves, her slenderness hadn't appeared to deter Luke. Far from it.

She stood quite still beneath the still-gushing shower, clutching her sponge to her breasts, oblivious to the water pelting her skin, oblivious to everything other than the heat stirring deep inside her body—a heat that made her face flush with shock and pain.

It was only the sudden damp warmth of her face that made her realise that she was crying.

And well she might, she acknowledged in anguish. She ought to cry for very shame that in her thoughts she had already committed self-betrayal, that in her thoughts she had shared with Luke those intimacies she was deceiving herself she had too much self-respect, too much pride, too high a moral code to share in actual practice.

Which was worse, she asked herself wearily later as she got dressed—to allow herself to imagine in the privacy of her most secret thoughts that she and Luke were lovers, and then to pretend to be angered and offended by the knowledge that he should want her merely as his sexual partner, or to admit honestly to herself that she wanted him, and to recklessly give herself to him, knowing that in doing so she was breaking every one of her self-made rules, and yet knowing at the same time that this was something she had to do, a need she had to appease, an experience she had to have? Was she really such a coward that she could allow herself the intimacy of Luke's body in the secret darkness of her thoughts, but could not permit that same intimacy in reality simply because it was not cloaked with words like 'love'?

In the end which of them was the more dishonest? Luke or herself? Shamingly, she already knew the answer.

Leo arrived rather later than expected. It was closer to lunchtime than just after breakfast when he drove up to the house in the Jaguar D-type vintage sports car that was his pride and joy, and he wasn't alone.

To her surprise, Natasha saw her aunt seated in the car next to him, her laughing face turned towards him, her hair windblown and tousled. For a moment Natasha was too surprised to speak, and watched in silence as Leo helped her aunt out of his car.

'Leo... Mr Rosenberg has brought me to see his gardens,' her aunt explained breathlessly as soon as she was within earshot. Her face was flushed with a pretty and unfamiliar colour which could have been caused by the breeziness of the open-topped car, but there was a sparkle in her eyes, a certain something in her manner as she turned to wait for Leo to lock the car and join them, that caused Natasha to wonder speculatively if there was rather more to her aunt's arrival than merely Leo's enthusiasm for renovating and restoring the house and its gardens.

'You see I took up your recommendation,' Leo announced as he joined them. 'And Helen has very kindly consented to come and give me the benefit of her advice——'

'I'm no expert,' Helen Lacey interrupted him. 'Merely an enthusiastic amateur.'

'A very gifted enthusiastic amateur,' Natasha put in.

'Extremely gifted,' Leo agreed. 'Having seen what you've achieved at Lacey Court, I must confess I'm rather reluctant to let you see how much the gardens here fall behind.'

'I'm sure you'd be far better advised by a qualified horticulturist or designer,' Natasha heard her aunt saying as the three of them fell into step. 'Although I must admit it is the kind of challenge I've always longed to take up.'

'Wait until you've seen the extent of the work that needs to be done,' Leo advised her. 'And our guests will expect to have such facilities as tennis-courts.'

'And croquet,' Helen advised him, 'especially if they're Americans. You've probably even got enough ground for a polo field as well. Now *that* would be a draw.'

'Polo,' Leo mused. 'It's very fashionable, of course.'

Listening to them, Natasha reflected rather wryly that they had almost forgotten she was with them, and she wondered if they were as aware as she was of how well they fell into step with one another, not just in practice as they walked towards the house together, but in theory as well, both of them equally enthusiastic about the house and its possibilities. Listening to them talk, she quickly realised that this could not possibly just be the first time they had met.

Her suspicions were confirmed over lunch, when Leo mentioned that he had called on her aunt immediately after his return from Amsterdam and they had had dinner together, followed by a lunch in town, when he had invited Helen up to London for the day to see his offices there.

Watching her aunt and Leo Rosenberg together, Natasha was suddenly aware of a devastatingly and totally unfamiliar sensation of aloneness, of longing... for what? she asked herself derisively. For Luke Templecombe?

While her aunt spent the afternoon exploring the garden and its possibilities, Natasha was closeted in the office with Leo as they went over her carefully prepared notes and schemes.

'These are ideal; just what I wanted,' Leo told her positively once they had finished.

'And the costings?' Natasha pressed anxiously, knowing that some of the fabrics she had chosen for the reception-rooms were expensive.

'Fine,' Leo assured her, adding, 'I might be a businessman, but I'm not a philistine, Natasha. I realise that the kind of quality we're discussing here doesn't come cheap, and nor should it. How soon could you start work here? The contractors are due to finish upstairs at the end of the month, and the sooner you can get started after that...'

Quickly Natasha assessed her present workload. She had several small commissions on hand which could either be completed or shelved to allow her to start work at the time Leo was requesting. Some time or other she would need to make a trip to Florence. Some of the fabrics she would like to use, not to mention the other decorative items she had included in her presentations, would mean a personal visit to the craftsmen concerned to check that what she wanted could be produced within her provisional budgets.

She explained all this to Leo, and waited hesitantly while he considered.

'I'd like to have the place ready for opening by Christmas, to catch the Christmas market which would be particularly lucrative.'

Christmas! Natasha took a deep breath. It would be pushing things a bit, and completion for that date would to a large extent be dependent on the ability and willingness of her Florentine contacts to provide her with what she wanted on time.

'I think I could manage it,' she told him cautiously. 'Depending on my suppliers. As far as the fabrics for the bedrooms are concerned, these will come from my father's factory, and I can virtually guarantee delivery on them, plus a good discount off normal prices, but for the fabrics for the reception areas, good though our stuff is, it cannot compare with the fabrics from Florence which I'd like to use, and I have no control over the supply date for those.'

'I understand,' Leo assured her, 'and I don't intend to have any penalty clauses added to our contract.'

He saw her surprise and smiled wryly, 'I trust my instincts in these things, Natasha, and any true entrepreneur who tells you he doesn't do the same thing is lying. My instincts tell me I can trust you— and not just because I'm already halfway towards

falling in love with your aunt,' he added with a grin
as he stood up.

Natasha gaped at him and he laughed again, a
little ruefully this time.

'She said you'd be shocked. I suppose to someone
of your age the very idea of a man in his fifties
falling in love——'

'No...no, you're wrong,' Natasha told him
quickly, and then admitted honestly, 'I was only
thinking this afternoon what a good couple the two
of you make. I just didn't expect you to——'

'To what? To admit that, having spent the years
since my wife's death telling myself that I'd never
want to marry again, I've suddenly discovered that
I was wrong. Life's too short to let pride stand in
the way of love and happiness; that's something I
*do* know. The moment I met your aunt, I realised
she was someone who was going to be important
to me. It was like having a light suddenly switched
on in a dark place in my life, illuminating its
darkness, warming its coldness. And I believe she
feels the same way about me.'

'Is that why you're giving me this contract?'
Natasha asked him hesitantly. 'Because you've
fallen in love with my aunt?'

He frowned at her. 'No. If I didn't think you
were up to the job, your relationship to Helen
wouldn't make the slightest difference.'

Listening to him, Natasha believed him and was
relieved. Much as she wanted the contract, she
wanted to earn it on her own merit and ability and
not for any other reason.

'I notice you've suggested several fabrics for the long gallery. As I said, a friend of mine is going to come down and advise me on the best placement of my art collection in the gallery, and I think I'd like a final decision about the fabric for the windows and the window-seats to come from him.'

Natasha nodded her head. The fabrics she had tentatively selected for the gallery were traditional tapestries in muted designs and colours to blend in with the old panelling—fabrics which would not detract from the main purpose of the panelled gallery which was to be a display case for the paintings Leo had collected, the majority of which he had already told her had been painted at the height of the Victorian mania for Gothic revival, and would thus be in keeping with the ambiance of the house.

'At the moment the paintings are in storage. I'm having them delivered here when the men have finished working on the gallery, which should be about the same time as they finish work on the bedrooms. We can make a decision about a fabric for the gallery then.'

Agreeing with him, Natasha smiled a little sadly to herself as she saw the way his gaze kept straying to the windows overlooking the garden. He was anxious to rejoin her aunt, Natasha could see, and so she diplomatically asked if he would mind if she went up to her own room to make a few telephone calls.

From her bedroom she could see down into the neglected kitchen garden, and that same earlier stab of awareness of her own single state knifed through her again as a quick glance through her window showed her the sight of Leo and her aunt walking arm in arm along one of the overgrown paths, stopping to study something, so deeply engrossed in one another that she automatically stepped back from the window, feeling that her observation of them, no matter how accidental, was somehow an intrusion into their privacy.

Alone, though, it was impossible to stop the demons of anguish tormenting her as she contrasted the closeness, the warmth, the mutuality of emotion and feeling between Leo and her aunt with the total lack of any such feelings which had characterised the interlude she had shared with Luke in her parents' garden. How appropriate that Leo's and her aunt's relationship should be shared with the warmth and light of the sun which bathed the garden, while hers with Luke had been cloaked and hidden in moonlight.

She tried to tell herself that she was glad she had escaped from him, but somehow, despite the ferocity of her thoughts, they had a hollow, unconvincing ring to them.

She didn't have any time alone with her aunt until just before the latter was about to leave.

The three of them had had dinner together, and now Leo was upstairs collecting some papers he needed prior to driving Helen back to Lacey Court on his way back to London.

Her work here was nearly finished for the time being, Natasha confirmed to her aunt. There was little more she could do until the workmen had finished, and she had made arrangements with

Leo's housekeeper that she would return for a few days at the end of the month just to check that she was still as satisfied with her plans, once she was able to study them in the context of the completed bedrooms.

'You'd better have a key, then,' the housekeeper told her. 'You'll be coming down on the bank-holiday weekend, and I shan't be here. I'm having a couple of weeks with my cousin in Bournemouth.'

'While we're on our own, there's something I think I should tell you,' her aunt murmured, as the housekeeper went in search of a spare key. 'We had a visitor yesterday, or rather *you* had a visitor.'

The kick of sensation that was pure visceral pleasure made Natasha tense her stomach muscles as she waited for her aunt to continue. Her mouth had gone dry, she discovered, and the tension invading her body made her feel as though she were poised like a diver on a high board.

'Was it . . . was it . . . ?'

'Luke Templecombe,' her aunt supplied drily for her. 'Yes, it was, and none too pleased to discover that the pigeon had fled the nest, so to speak. Unfortunately when he arrived I wasn't there, and when I came in your mother had already told him where you were.'

Her heart gave a tremendous bound, a sharp sensation of excitement quickly followed by an equally intense feeling of sickness that made it impossible for her to do anything other than stare at her aunt while the colour came and went in her face.

'I agree with you, he *is* a very dangerous young man, all the more so because he is also so very intensely male. He wants you, Natasha, and something tells me he isn't going to be put off by this tale you've told him about there being someone else. It might even add spice to the game.'

'Yes,' Natasha agreed tonelessly. Her betraying burst of euphoria had faded into a miasma of anguish and misery. 'But that's all it is to him . . . a game . . .'

'Meaning what?' her aunt asked gently. 'That to you it's something more?'

Natasha shook her head. 'Not yet, but it could be if I let him——' She bit her lip and corrected grimly, 'If I allowed myself to . . .'

'To take him as your lover?'

'I was going to say to become involved with him. Oh, it's hopeless . . . useless.' She swung round miserably. 'I can't understand why I should want him the way I do. He's everything I most dislike in the male sex: cold, cynical, unable to react to any woman other than as a sexual object.'

'It's called sexual attraction,' her aunt told her drily, 'and, make no mistake about it, it's a very potent force. If it's any consolation to you, I got the impression that he resents it just as much as you do. I could tell from his expression that he bitterly resented having to ask where you were. He's an intelligent man, Natasha; he'll have guessed exactly why you're running from him. He'll know quite well that if this supposed commitment of yours to someone else meant a damn there'd be no need for you to run.'

'He thinks I'm a sexually experienced woman with a list of lovers behind me as long as his own,' Natasha told her despairingly. 'Even if I were to...to allow things to develop...how could I tell him? How could I explain?'

'That you lied to him to save Emma's hide? You might be surprised. He might——'

'What? Be thrilled out of his mind to discover that I'm still a virgin?' She shook her head. 'This isn't fantasy, Helen, it's reality. He doesn't want me for my ignorance and lack of experience because they involve responsibilities he doesn't want to take on. He wants someone who can match him on his own ground...someone who knows the rules...someone whom he can discard as easily as he picked up once he's grown bored.'

'And what do you want, Tasha?' her aunt asked her softly. 'Do you know?'

Natasha grimaced.

'Not really. I want him, physically, very badly indeed, and believe me, just admitting *that* takes as much courage as I have. I can't begin to tell you what admitting it has done to my self-esteem. I thought I was above that kind of sexual need. I thought——'

'That you weren't *human*. My dear, all of us are that. If it's really that bad, if you really desire him so intensely, why not——'

'Have an affair with him? How can I without explaining...without betraying——?' She bit her lip. 'No, it's impossible.'

'Nothing's ever impossible,' her aunt reminded her warningly, 'but, if it's any consolation to you, he has left Sutton Minster and gone back to

London. I saw Lucille Templecombe yesterday and she told me that he'd gone——'

She broke off as the housekeeper came back triumphantly carrying a spare set of keys.

'I'll have to check with Leo, of course, but I'm sure he won't mind.'

'What won't I mind?' Leo asked, walking into the hall, and in the general stir of explanations and arrangements Natasha was able to push Luke Templecombe to the back of her mind.

But not for long. She was leaving Stonelovel Manor in the morning to return home, and once her aunt and Leo were gone and she was back upstairs, laboriously checking through her list of suppliers to ensure that she had all the details she was going to need when the time came to make firm orders, she found herself sitting staring into space instead of working, trying to damp down the fierce, searing heart-burning inside her at the thought of Luke coming in search of her . . . and finding her . . . Her defences were pitifully weak—so weak that he would have no trouble in breaching them if he chose to do so, and the worst of it was that more than half of her wished that he might do so, that he *might* take the burden of decision from her and commit her to the course that her rebellious flesh longed to take.

Wryly, she acknowledged that she was in for another sleepless night.

## CHAPTER EIGHT

MORNING had arrived, but Luke had not, and today Natasha was due to leave the manor and return home. She told herself that she was glad that Luke had chosen not to put in an appearance, to test her will-power, to defy her denial of her need for him, but she knew that it wasn't entirely true.

It still shocked her that she should feel this intensity of desire, this awesome, enervating, sharp physical need, but slowly she was coming to accept it as fact, to even test out its alienness by surreptitiously studying the workmen who were still busy on the house, but despite the plethora of male muscles and sexuality, despite the keenly interested scrutiny she had received from more than one pair of male eyes while she had been checking out the layout of the new bedrooms, no sharp *frisson* of sensation had stirred her body, no erotic awareness of them as male and herself as female, no aching, painful need like the one that Luke had made her feel, and she wasn't sure whether to be relieved or disappointed by this discovery.

It was late afternoon when she finally got in her car and set out for home, unwillingly admitting to herself that she had perhaps deliberately delayed her departure, just in case Luke should put in an appearance.

Fool, she derided herself, as she drove home. Common sense told her that her aunt was wrong in believing that Luke intended to seek her out. Why should he? Even she with her lack of experience could see that he was the kind of man who would never go short of female companionship. Why should he bother to pursue her?

It was a surprise when she got home to discover that her aunt wasn't there.

'I can't understand her,' Natasha's own mother complained. 'Since she's met this...this man she seems to have changed completely. She never used to want to go anywhere, and now...well, we hardly ever see her. When I asked her how long she was going to be away, she said that she really didn't know, that Leo had business in New York, and that they would probably fly from there to Switzerland.'

'Stop fussing, my dear,' Natasha's father intervened. 'Helen is old enough to know her own mind. Personally I'm only too pleased to see her taking an interest in life again.'

'She *did* have an interest in life. She had the garden,' was Natasha's mother's slightly peevish comment.

Natasha repressed a sympathetic sigh, suspecting that her mother was missing the close companionship the two of them had shared.

'Leo really is very nice,' she comforted her mother, 'and he's as good as told me that he's in love with Helen.'

'Well, I suppose she does deserve some happiness. She's been alone long enough.' Natasha watched as her mother gave a small shiver, and looked across at her own husband. 'If the two of them develop a permanent relationship, though, I'm going to miss her.'

'Me, too,' Natasha agreed, and then lightened the slightly sombre tone of the conversation by adding, 'I know someone who won't, though— Richard's mother. She blames Helen for the supremacy of our garden.'

'Oh, yes, that reminds me, Natasha. Someone called here asking for you while you were away— Richard's cousin, a very handsome young man.'

'Yes, Helen told me,' Natasha said neutrally, trying to keep her voice as calm as possible, but sensing that her father wasn't altogether deceived, from the thoughtful look he gave her. Anxious to get off the dangerous subject of Luke Templecombe just as quickly as she could, she turned to her father and said quickly, 'If you've got some time to spare, I'd like to go over the schemes Leo's agreed for the bedrooms at the manor. We'll be using the company's fabrics for the bedrooms, although I'm going to need some special lots dyeing to accommodate the full colour ranges I want to use. Leo will get the full discount on the lines we already run, but he understands that the special orders will cost more.' She went on to explain to her father that, wherever possible, the original features of the house had been retained so that some of the guest bedrooms had their original panelling, while others had had items such as wardrobes and other necessities put in, including the new partition walls hidden behind new panelling, most of which had been left in its natural state and then limed to achieve a soft, weathered silvery finish.

It was for these rooms that Natasha needed the special dye runs of fabric, knowing that they would need slightly softer colours than the very rich shades the company normally produced.

'Does this man—Leo—does he intend to live in the house or——?'

'Oh, yes, he's retained the small, original wing for his own use. It's beautiful: five bedrooms, three each with their own bathrooms, plus the most marvellous original panelled gallery overlooking the enclosed kitchen garden, which he intends to keep for his own private use. That was why I put him in touch with Helen. He was complaining that he couldn't find anyone to advise him on replanning and replanting the gardens. That reminds me,' she added, turning to her father, 'I'm going to need to make another trip to Florence some time in the near future, so if there's anything you want while I'm over there... I know exactly the fabrics I want for the long gallery—something which isn't going to detract from the paintings Leo intends to have hung on the walls, and yet which is rich enough to set off the panelling and the stucco ceiling...'

Natasha had eight hectic days plus one full weekend in which to clear her desk and her outstanding commissions, before she had to return to the manor. This necessitated her working well into the evenings and her free weekend as well, but she didn't mind.

The hard work helped to stop her thinking about Luke—well, almost... She was past the stage now of expecting to hear his voice each time the phone rang, past the stage of experiencing that savage thrill of fear-cum-excitement at the thought of seeing or speaking to him.

She told herself that it was for the best that he hadn't got in touch with her, that her most sensible course of action by far was to put him completely out of her mind and out of her life. She told herself as well that one day there would come a time when she would look back on the whole incident and marvel at her own idiocy and the narrowness of her escape from a situation which could only damage both her self-esteem and her self-respect, but she still avoided walking in the gardens at night; she still found it hard to sleep. She still felt her body tense with something that wasn't entirely dread when the phone rang or someone knocked on her street door.

On the Thursday afternoon preceding the bank-holiday weekend, she packed for her return journey to the manor, intending to leave a little earlier than she had originally planned in order to avoid the early holiday traffic.

The weather forecast for the weekend was promising good weather, which meant that the roads were bound to be busy. Never an entirely happy driver in heavy traffic at the best of times, Natasha had no wish to be caught up in queues of impatient and thus perhaps over-reckless drivers.

She arrived at Stonelovel just as the housekeeper was on the point of leaving. The older woman looked flustered and hot, and obviously didn't want to be delayed.

As she stepped into the waiting taxi, she called out to Natasha, 'Oh, by the way, I've put you in the same room. I hope that's all right. There's plenty of food in the fridge.'

Thanking her, Natasha unlocked the door and went inside.

The house seemed oddly quiet after the busy hum of workmen. The air in the hall was still full of dust. It floated in the sunlight pouring in through the now renovated and uncovered leaded windows on the stairs.

What she really ought to do first was to unpack her car, but the impulse to walk through the now empty rooms and inspect them at her leisure was far too tempting, Natasha acknowledged.

Work was still in progress on some of the reception-rooms, but for the first time Natasha was now able to see some distinct resemblance between the detailed architect's drawing Leo had shown her and the rooms themselves.

Everything in the house that was original had been meticulously and carefully restored, huge fireplaces uncovered, having been hidden behind centuries of 'improvements', panelling freed from its clogging coats of paint, plaster ceilings revealed by the removal of lowered false ceilings.

In the end she spent far longer than she had anticipated slowly going from room to room, picturing them as they had been in her mind's eye from the photographs Leo had taken of the house when he first took it over and marvelling at what had been achieved in such a relatively short space of time.

It helped having the money to be able to employ expert craftspeople, she acknowledged, but money on its own wasn't enough...without Leo's enthusiasm...his love for the house...

Her imagination took fire as she explored, mentally clothing the rooms in the fabrics she had already chosen.

The discovery that it was almost eight o'clock in the evening and that she had spent several hours lost in the magic of bringing to life these empty rooms forced her to abandon them and return to her car to collect her things.

As she carried them upstairs, she wondered wryly if it was the euphoria of realising almost for the first time how confident she actually felt about achieving the effects Leo wanted, of discovering, when she admired the handiwork of the craftsmen responsible for the restoration of the house, that she too was part of that same team, *her* skills equal in Leo's eyes at least to theirs...or if it was simply the fact that she hadn't eaten anything since her late breakfast and was therefore extremely hungry.

Hungry, but too euphoric, too restless to settle down to anything so mundane as preparing a meal. Fortunately the housekeeper had stocked the refrigerator thoughtfully and generously—there was a large cold cooked chicken, plus a wide variety of salads, fruits and vegetables—and, slightly guiltily telling herself that she would make up for her laziness in the morning, Natasha made herself a thick chicken sandwich using wholemeal bread and several slices off the chicken.

What she needed to do now, she told herself firmly as she ate it and drank a cup of coffee, sitting at the kitchen table, was to go out and have a pleasant relaxing walk through the grounds to bring herself down into a less elevated state.

Tomorrow she could throw herself thoroughly into her work; tonight she needed a good night's sleep. Tonight, if she dreamed of anything, she wanted those dreams to be of fabrics, not of Luke Templecombe. He had already disturbed far too many of her nights...and far too many of her days.

Having quickly washed up, she opened the back door and stepped outside. It had been a warm day, and the air was now pleasantly cool, refreshing enough to make her want to breathe in deep lungfuls of it, and yet not so chilly that she needed to go back inside to find something warm to put on over her jeans and Tshirt.

Knowing that she was going to be the only occupant of the house, she had only brought with her a handful of casual clothes, the kind she felt most comfortable in while working: old worn jeans, comfortable baggy sweaters. She nearly always bought men's jumpers, liking their length and generosity. In the winter it was cold upstairs at the top of her house in her workroom and she generally wore them over the top of thermal vests, plus warm shirts to retain her body heat. In summer they were equally effective over something thinner.

It would be relaxing now to walk round the kitchen garden and to exercise her overactive brain in imagining what it might be transformed into with her aunt's skill.

The house, built in the reign of Charles II, would just about have been settling into its surroundings when his niece Mary married her Dutchman. It was during that period that the vogue for gardens composed of vistas, contained in yew hedges, for topiary work, and for neatly designed beds, of the type which in France were known as parterres, had been at its height.

At Lacey Court they had a knot garden designed by her aunt which made use of two different shades of green hedging which was universally admired, but here in this walled kitchen garden her aunt would have so much more scope for her skills. How lucky she was loving not just the man, but his home, and on top of that to be granted the munificence of such a wonderful professional challenge as well.

Not that anyone deserved that happiness more than her aunt. It was completely wrong of her to feel so...so what? Envious...of another's happiness? She stopped walking abruptly, instinctively turning her face towards the shadows, even though there was no one else there to read her expression.

Since meeting Luke Templecombe, she felt as though her whole life had been turned upside-down, as though she had been forced to confront facets of herself she had never previously realised existed, facets she wasn't entirely at ease with.

Driven by the restlessness that possessed her, she walked out of the walled garden, following a path which she knew led through the gardens to the perimeter of the estate and from there to join a pathway, now overgrown in many places, which ran along the inside of the boundary fence.

It was later than she had expected when she eventually got back. Almost midnight, in fact, and, although she felt physically exhausted, mentally she was as alert and on edge as ever.

She went upstairs to have a bath and prepare for bed, and it was just as she was stepping out of the bath that she saw the sweeping illumination of a car's headlights coming down the drive.

Puzzled rather than alarmed, she dried herself quickly, and then pulled on her discarded outer clothes. It could only be Leo returning unexpectedly at this hour, and she had bolted and barred the doors, preventing him from getting in. She knew that, even if he noticed the omission of her underwear, he was hardly likely to comment on it. She had witnessed the way he looked at her aunt, heard him describe his feelings for her, and had known that they were genuine.

Running quickly downstairs, she headed for the main entrance hall just as he reached the door from the other side. She heard him inserting his key, and called out to him, 'I've bolted the door from the inside, Leo. I'll just open it for you... You're lucky I was in,' she added. 'I'd virtually only just got back from a long walk and I was in the bath when I saw your car headlights.'

She was smiling welcomingly as she slid back the final bolt and unsnapped the lock so that she could open the door. As she did so, the light from the hallway spilled outside illuminating the man standing there. Immediately her smile died, to be replaced by disbelief and a shocked wave of intense awareness that burned up in a tide of colour, crimsoning her skin.

'Luke,' she whispered, faltering, instinctively stepping back as he came forward, her eyes wide with apprehension and shock. 'You shouldn't have come here,' she told him huskily as he came into the hall and closed the door behind him. 'I told you I didn't want to see you again. You've made a mistake if you——'

'I'm afraid *you're* the one who's made a mistake,' came the laconic reply. 'I haven't come here looking for you, Natasha.'

The shock of his casual, uncaring disclaimer silenced her, freezing her ability to reason or think— to say anything beyond a stammered and defensive, 'Then why *are* you here? You——'

'Leo asked me to come down and check over this gallery of his, to advise him on the placing of his collection, and this is the first opportunity I've had to do so.'

Sickly Natasha stared at him, her skin burning with chagrin and embarrassment as she realised that he was telling the truth. Why oh, why had she assumed that he had come here in pursuit of her? Why on earth hadn't she kept her mouth shut, let him explain his appearance?

'Leo didn't say anything to me,' she said, turning her back on him and missing the narrow-eyed scrutiny he gave her.

'No. Well, maybe he didn't think it important. I take it that visitors are still sleeping upstairs on the third floor?'

Still keeping her back to him, Natasha nodded. 'There's no one here but me,' she told him awkwardly.

'Yes, Leo did mention that the place would be empty apart from the designer he'd hired. Stupid of me, perhaps, but I never made the connection between that comment and yourself.'

Natasha felt her face burn anew. A none too subtle reminder of her idiotically self-betraying assumption that he had come in search of her.

'It's late,' she said jerkily. 'I was just on my way to bed.'

'So I see,' he murmured as she turned round. His glance was resting on the soft, unrestrained thrust of her breasts beneath her bulky top and Natasha had a momentary and far too telling awareness of how it had felt to have his hands and then his mouth caressing their softness.

She drew in a sharp, unstable breath. Hadn't she made enough of a fool of herself already tonight, without compounding that stupidity? The last thing she wanted now was for Luke to become aware of her reaction to him.

'I thought you were Leo,' she snapped defensively, as though answering an unspoken question, and then watched uncertainly as something happened to the bones of his face, compressing them somehow so that the air of relaxed mockery died from his eyes and was replaced by a hard, penetrating sharpness that took her breath away and made her stomach clench in silent agony.

'Did you, now?' he said softly. 'I'm sorry I disappointed you.'

'So am I,' she retorted recklessly, and without giving him any opportunity to retaliate she fled, hoping that her exit in the direction of the stairs looked a lot more controlled and self-possessed than it felt.

Luke here... She couldn't believe it. It was like something out of the very worst of her night-mares—or the very best of her daydreams. She shuddered a little at the knowledge of her own contrary feelings. Luke here...Luke sleeping under the same roof. How long did he intend to stay? How long?

Much to her own surprise, having been convinced that the knowledge that Luke was sharing the same roof with her would mean yet another restless night, not only did she sleep exceptionally well, but she actually managed to oversleep as well, waking up to find the sun shining into her room.

The house felt quiet and empty, as though there was no one else in it apart from herself, as though at some time during the night Luke had left.

Angrily she quelled the sharp stab of pain caused by that thought. If he *had* left, she ought to be relieved, not disappointed. However, when she went downstairs, there was a note on the immaculately clean kitchen table, reading simply, 'Am working in the long gallery. Perhaps you could spare the time to show me the fabric samples Leo tells me you have selected for the windows.'

It was only natural of course that he should want to make sure that she wasn't thinking of using some totally unsuitable fabric which might completely ruin the atmosphere of the gallery and draw the eye away from the paintings, but her professional pride was scorched with resentment that he should make it so obvious that he might want to veto her suggestions.

She wondered what time he had started work. It must have been early. She herself was no stranger to working long hours and making early starts. She wondered if he perhaps thought that she made a habit of lying in bed until the morning was half over, and once again her professional pride revolted.

She made herself some filter coffee and found a grapefruit in the fridge, rejecting the temptation to skip breakfast, knowing that the amount of work which lay ahead of her might mean that she had to miss lunch. It was always the same—once she got involved in her work, she tended to resent any interruption which took her away from it.

The coffee was hot and reviving and, on an impulse she didn't want to examine too closely, she poured out two more mugs of it, carrying them with her on a tray as she made her way to the gallery, stopping off first in Leo's office to collect the samples she had left there the previous evening.

When she opened the door to the gallery, Luke was standing surrounded by half-open packing cases, hands on his hips, a frown darkening his eyes.

He looked up briefly as she walked in and, ignoring the sharp tightening sensation that coiled through her body, Natasha said as calmly as she could, 'I thought you might like a cup of coffee.

I've brought my samples with me, and once you're ready to look at them...'

Several of the paintings had already been removed from their crates and she looked curiously at them as she put the tray down on the floor.

Watching her, Luke said drily, 'If you're wondering how much they're worth, I can assure you that Leo has made a very good investment.'

Natasha was astounded, as much by the cynicism in his voice as by his comment, and she swung round, forgetting to be cautious and on her guard as she said in surprise, 'Why should I be in the least bit interested in their material value? I was simply curious about them, that's all. Naturally, from a professional point of view——'

She stopped as she saw the way his mouth twisted.

'Professional. Is that what you consider yourself to be?' Luke taunted her. 'You get your latest lover to let you play at decorating his new acquisition and on the strength of that you consider yourself professional.'

Natasha was astounded—so astounded that for a moment she couldn't do anything other than stare at him with her mouth open, and then, realising how idiotic she must look, she snapped it closed and said through gritted teeth, 'For your information, Leo is not my lover, and even if he were...even if he were...I do not need to...to have sex with my potential clients in order to get their business. And as for not being professional...'

She lifted her head and stared proudly and furiously at him.

'All right. So maybe I don't have any paper qualifications, and certainly normally I would not be taking on a commission as large as this one. I'm not a designer and have never pretended to be. But I *do* know about fabric, especially the kind of fabrics Leo wants for this house. That's why he contacted me in the first place. However, if you, with your wealth of experience and knowledge of these things, feel that he'd be better served employing some fashionable interior design house, then no doubt you'll tell him so. Right now it isn't your personal and prejudiced views of my qualifications for this job that I want, but simply your views on the fabrics I've selected for the furnishings here in the gallery.'

Without giving him any chance to intervene, she swept on, carried away by the hot swell of rage and, yes, pain as well, that moved so powerfully within her.

She had always known that he despised her, even more, she suspected, than he had desired her...but it had been as a woman that she had thought that he had held this contempt for her...not as a human being.

What did he know of her skill or lack of it?

She said as much, throwing the question at him like a challenge, and then confronting him, breathless, and more angry than she could virtually ever remember being.

'I saw Jake Pendraggon's Cornish house featured in a magazine article,' he told her drily. 'Whoever wrote the article was discreet, saying merely that the place had been decorated by a close friend of Mr Pendraggon's, but it isn't difficult to put two and two together.'

'To make five,' Natasha told him through gritted teeth. 'I did not decorate Jake's house, and neither am I having an affair with Leo. In fact——'

'Prove it,' he interrupted quietly, so quietly that for a moment she thought she must have misheard him, but then he repeated, 'Prove it by having dinner with me tonight.'

Have dinner with him? What on earth would that prove? Not that she felt the need to prove anything to him—anything at all. But that was a lie, she acknowledged, as she looked from his face, set into an expression of cynical awareness that she would refuse his invitation, to the samples she was still holding in her hand. She *did* need to prove something to him. She wanted him to acknowledge that her skill in her own field was worthy of recognition and praise; she wanted to see the cynicism die out of his eyes, to be replaced by... by what? Respect!

Prove it, he had challenged, and of course she was far too mature, far too sensible to give in to that kind of emotional pressure, and yet still she heard herself saying recklessly and shakily, 'All right, I will, but only if you'll stop treating me as though I'm going to drape this place with hundreds of yards of totally unsuitable chintz and fussy bows, and instead look at these samples I've chosen—if not with a totally unbiased eye, then at least with the closest you can manage to one. I realise that you don't like... that you want to...'

To think the worst of me, she had been about to say, but he substituted for her before she could do so.

'That I desire you physically. Yes. Inconvenient, isn't it? For both of us. And don't pretend you don't know what I mean, that you aren't equally turned on by me as I am by you. You daren't let yourself come within five yards of me, and I feel exactly the same way about you. The simplest solution would be for us to have sex with one another right here and now, and get the whole thing over and done with. Both of us know quite well that, once the itch has been scratched, once we've exorcised whatever need it is that has attacked us so inconveniently, it will die as quickly as it flared into life, but woman-like of course you can't be honest enough to face reality. You want me just as much as I want you but——'

Natasha stared at him in stupefaction, the colour slowly fading from her skin and then rushing back in a low wave of mortification.

'I do not want you,' she snapped frantically at him. 'And the reason I don't want to...to come too close to you is...is that I like my own personal space remaining uninvaded...by anyone.'

'You're lying,' Luke told her flatly. 'But have it your own way. I'll tell you this, though—if you think that by playing coy and hard to get you're going to get me chasing after you, you can think again. I never play those kinds of games.'

'No, I don't suppose you do,' Natasha agreed. Suddenly she was cold, a deep, biting, inward cold which had nothing to do with the temperature. 'You like to play your own game, by your own rules, don't you, Luke? But here's one woman who isn't going to join that game.' And then recklessly, because suddenly she was so tired, so sickened, so miserably aware of how foolish she had been in even allowing into her most private thoughts the kind of idiotic fantasy which had led her into believing that somewhere beneath the hardness, beneath the cynicism, beneath the tough outer shell lay a real human being, with real emotions, and real desires, she told him shakily, 'I can't change the way you think of me, Luke. I don't even *want* to, but I will tell you this. No matter what you do think, you don't know me. Yes, I desire you. Yes, I want to make love with you—and I choose those words deliberately, not out of some kind of stupid, self-deceiving emotionalism because I need them to cloak a physical need in some kind of disguise, but because for me that's what any physical act of intimacy between two people must have.'

'Are you trying to tell me that if I lied to you, if I told you I loved you, if I wrapped up my need in pretty, meaningless words, you'd go to bed with me?'

'No,' she told him firmly and truthfully. 'I know you don't love me, and I admit that doesn't stop me wanting you, but you're talking about that wanting, that desire as though it's something you resent—some weakness for which you can only feel contempt. Perhaps I *am* naïve, stupid, self-deceptive, but I believe that even when there is no "love" as described by the poets and writers between two people, there can still be tenderness, caring, mutual respect, laughter, pleasure and a true giving...of wanting to give and to please. But of course for that both people concerned would need to be well-adjusted, mature human beings, with the capacity to see the foibles and weaknesses of themselves and of others, and yet be able to live with them, to feel compassion and understanding for them...and we both know that you can never feel like that, Luke—not while you're still a little boy, hating your mother for leaving you, unable to understand what could have motivated her, wanting to punish her and to go on punishing her and totally unable to see beyond your own needs to hers. Here.' She walked up to him and shoved the samples towards him, not bothering to see if he picked them up or let them fall.

'These are the fabrics I thought most suitable for in here, depending on the colours of the paintings and their frames. I've deliberately tried to choose those which will fade graciously into the background, rather than clamour for attention. If you don't approve of them, I suggest you take it up with Leo. Now I'm afraid I have work to do.'

As she walked towards the door, she prayed she would get there without collapsing. She was in shock, she recognised, as she opened the door. It was shock that had made her react like that, berate him like that, and yet, she acknowledged as she opened the door and passed through it, she had spoken the truth as she saw it.

Even so, her tender heart ached for the look she had seen momentarily and so painfully in his eyes when she had accused him of still hating his mother,

of resenting her for deserting him and, because of
that, punishing her sex by holding it in contempt.
He was an intelligent man, and one who must have
already seen in himself this schism, this vulnerability. He hadn't needed her to point it out to him.

# CHAPTER NINE

FOR the rest of the day, Natasha made sure that she kept out of Luke's way.

She was angry with him and angry with herself as well, and yet underneath that anger ran a deep vein of compassion for him ... pity almost. A pity that she knew quite well he would not want.

She had seen so illuminatingly in those self-betraying words of his the reality of what his physical desire for her meant to him, the paucity and worthlessness of it, and had discovered that despite her own pain, her own anguish in wanting this man, in loving this man who, she now recognised shockingly and far, far too late, could not and would not want to share those feelings, she still felt that of the two of them he was the worse off. How truly appalling it must be never to be able to allow oneself to feel anything for another human being other than that cold, clinical desire only tempered to heat by dislike and contempt. No, despite her own anguish at recognising what she suspected she had always known—that her own physical desire for him was only one part of a complex range of emotions and needs, which for convenience's sake the human psyche lumped together under the word 'love'—she would not have wanted to change places with him, to experience the cold inner emptiness that he must suffer, that he *had* to suffer in the knowledge that, no matter what the emotions of his partner in any sexual intimacy, all he could feel in return was physical satisfaction and emotional sterility.

Half of her urged her to pack her things and leave the house, now before there were any more confrontations between them, but the other half said stubbornly that she had work to do and that to leave now would surely be to confirm to Luke that she was, as he had so sneeringly told her, lacking in professionalism. And so she stayed, working at an exhausting pace, trying to banish from her mind the knowledge that Luke was in the house with her, trying to force herself to believe that she was completely alone, but every now and again her defences broke down, and she would sit staring into space, confronting the unwanted knowledge that she loved him as well as desired him. She had known it irrevocably in that moment when she had flung her accusations at him, and had then looked into his eyes and seen the shocked confusion darkening them, like a child cruelly and wantonly hurt by the uncaring actions of an adult. In that moment she had ached to go to him, to hold him, to protect and cherish, not just the man, but the child within him as well, in the age-old way of women in love.

She loved Luke Templecombe; she shivered in the thrill of horror that iced her spine. There was only one way to deal with such an all-encompassing, idiotic folly, and that was to shut herself off from it, to starve it of her thoughts, her attention, her concern, to resolutely ignore what she felt in the hope that without the nourishment of wanton hope and desire it would slowly die. Slowly and painfully, she acknowledged, shivering again. Did she have the strength to endure that kind of pain? Did she have any alternative other than to do so?

Not really.

At six o'clock, she stopped work, recognising that if she did not eat soon she would probably not eat at all.

She opened the kitchen door cautiously, relieved to discover that the room was empty, and then left it open so that if Luke should decide to come down here he would realise she was there and go away again. He must, she recognised, have as little desire to see her as she had him.

She tried not to remember that he had asked her out to dinner, tried not to fantasise about where such an invitation might have led.

It would potentially of course have led to his bed, but once there, no matter how much physical pleasure he might have given her, emotionally he would have destroyed her. Not because he didn't love her—there could still have been tenderness between them, respect, pleasure and a thousand other positive emotions—but because he had shown her so clearly how he viewed, not just her, but the whole of her sex, and she had known then that for her no amount of sexual expertise could cancel out that deep inner contempt, that basic lack that would have meant he was rejecting her as a person, even at the very moment when he possessed her most intimately.

Without much enthusiasm, she made herself a cold meat salad, and sat down to eat it at the kitchen table.

She was halfway through it when Luke walked in. Immediately she stiffened, her throat closing up against the wave of emotion that struck her.

His jeans were coated with a film of dust; she could smell it on his skin, and see the way it was ingrained into the flesh of his throat and face as he came towards her.

She saw the way his mouth tightened as he looked down at her half-eaten meal. A man's mouth said so much about him. Luke's was sharply defined, mobile, the full curve of his bottom lip openly sensual. She focused on it for a handful of seconds too long, suddenly aware that she felt oddly dizzy.

'I take it, then, that you won't be having dinner with me tonight, after all.'

The mockery in his voice brought her back to reality. She dragged her attention away from his mouth and retaliated wryly, 'Something tells me that everything you do or say has its price, Luke, and I'm afraid that no meal, however excellent, would be worth the payment I suspect you'd ask.

She watched as mockery gave way to disbelief and then anger.

'If you're seriously suggesting that I'd expect you to go to bed with me simply because I'd bought you a meal...'

She could see that he was furious with her, but recklessly she didn't care. Let him see what it felt like to be insulted and treated with contempt.

'I'll have you know that I am not the kind of man who expects a woman to pay for a meal with her body.'

'And neither am I the kind of woman who has sex with a man for no other reason than that she feels fleeting physical desire for him,' Natasha retaliated. She pushed aside her half-eaten meal and stood up. 'It's been a long day, and I'm tired, Luke.'

As she started to walk past him, he said curtly, 'Wait.'

Involuntarily she stopped.

'You left these in the gallery,' he told her, handing her her samples of fabric.

She took them from him automatically, flinching as her fingers brushed his skin, dazed by the knowledge that even such a brief physical contact could stir her emotions so deeply. It was hard not to imagine what she would feel like given the freedom to touch him more intimately, to explore the male shaping of him, to feel the aroused movement of flesh and muscle...

He was already turning away from her, making her shakily relieved that he couldn't read her mind.

As she turned towards the door, she heard him saying almost gruffly, 'I owe you an apology, by the way. No one without an excellent knowledge of the period and its furnishings could have chosen those particular fabrics. There's one there—a tapestry in a similar shade to the panelling...'

For a moment Natasha was almost too stunned to speak. He was apologising, actually apologising, and more—admitting that she had knowledge, that she had skill. She knew very well that she ought not to let his words go to her head like wine, that she ought to suppress the delighted euphoria bubbling inside her, that it was ridiculous that she should feel pleasure, gratitude almost, in his reluctant words of praise. It was all she could do to say sedately, 'Yes, I know the one you mean. I liked that too, but of course the final choice depends on Leo's views. I had hoped to narrow it down to say three or four fabrics, but first I'd need to see the paintings and their frames.'

'I've virtually unpacked them all now. I've got a layout planned as to how and where they should be hung, but until they are I doubt that you'll be able to make any firm decision. It's going to be a couple of days at least before I get to that stage.'

'That's all right,' Natasha told him. 'I've plenty of work to be going on with in the meantime.'

Was he hinting that she ought to leave? Or was she becoming oversensitive? She decided that she was. After all, it couldn't matter to him whether she stayed or not. Now that she had made it plain that she wanted far more from a relationship than he was ever likely to offer, she doubted that he would continue to want her.

She was just turning away from him when he said abruptly, 'Natasha, I owe you another apology. I should never have implied that you got this contract because you were sleeping with Leo.'

'No, you shouldn't,' she agreed shakily.

'Not prepared to accept my apology?' he queried, watching her. 'Well, I suppose I can't blame you for that. Physical desire can lead a man into all manner of folly, and I suspect that today I've just about run the whole range of them. I'd like us to make a fresh start—forget everything that's happened. Will you do that, Tasha? Will you have dinner with me tonight, just as though we are two people who have just met, and having just met both want to discover a little more about one another? There won't be any strings, I promise you that. I haven't yet reached the stage of having to trick women into going to bed with me.'

She could well believe it. Logic, common sense, self-protection urged her to refuse, urged her to remember that, although he had apologised, nothing had really changed. He was still the same man he had been this morning...still the same man who had made it so painfully plain to her just what he thought of her and of the rest of her sex, and yet disturbingly she heard herself saying, 'Just as long as you realise that it will only be as two colleagues that we're dining together, Luke, and not as two potential lovers.'

What on earth had she done? she asked herself shakily when she got to her room. Why on earth had she agreed, exposed herself to further danger, further pain? She had no answers, only an intense aching desire to be with him...to share something with him, even if it could only be her enthusiasm for her work. And if he should break his word, if he should try to persuade her... Well, then she would just have to tell him the truth, she decided recklessly—or at least enough of it to make sure that he would not make love to her.

*　　*　　*

She suspected she knew exactly how to do that. She would simply tell him that she was a virgin, that she was not, as he had obviously assumed, a woman of experience and sexual knowledge. Once he knew that, once he realised how little physical pleasure and how much emotional danger there could be for him in his possession of her, he would cease pursuing her. Sadly she recognised the truth that her innocence, her total commitment both emotional and physical, which another man might have cherished and revered, were both unnecessary and unwanted as far as Luke's desire for her was concerned. To him they would be burdens he would not want to assume, and the mere knowledge that they existed would be sufficient to kill any lingering desire he might have for her.

She had only brought casual clothes with her, but there was after all no need for her to dress up... to impress or please, to tantalise or arouse. In the end she opted for a plain cotton skirt in soft cotton stretch jersey teamed with a white sleeveless polo-necked top. The outfit looked and felt cool, and, she felt, covered enough of her body to make it plain to Luke that she was not covertly trying to attract him.

He was waiting for her when she went downstairs. Like her he had showered and changed. They looked at one another almost equally warily, she recognised, as he opened the front door for her and waited until she had locked it behind her.

'I've booked a table at a small place only a few miles away. It's on the river, and they specialise in fresh-water fish dishes. I should have checked first that you do like fish.'

'I do,' Natasha assured him, waiting while he unlocked his car and then opened the passenger door for her. He was careful not to touch her any more than was strictly necessary, and she sensed that he was deliberately distancing himself from her sexually. Let's start again, he had said . . . But start again to what purpose? As he set the powerful car in motion, she reminded herself that he had not forced her to accept his invitation and that she was here with him by her own decision.

He made some comment about the countryside around the house, and she responded in kind.

'Leo is thrilled with the house,' she offered tentatively, trying to follow his example and make innocuous small talk. 'He told me he fell in love with it the moment he saw it.'

'Yes. For all his astuteness where business matters are concerned, Leo is a romantic at heart, and I'm afraid people are somewhat inclined to take advantage of that fact once they recognise it.'

A hint that he believed that *she* might try to do so? Natasha shot him a wary look. He was concentrating on his driving, his profile hard, sombre almost. She realised with a small shock that she had never seen him smile—not properly, not with real warmth—and that knowledge saddened her.

The restaurant was, as Luke had told her, only a short distance away, its car park already almost full. As she got out of the car, Natasha could hear the murmur of the river, blending with people's voices.

'It is possible to dine outside,' Luke told her, guiding her across the car park, 'but I thought it would be more comfortable, if less romantic, inside.'

Natasha shot him another wary look, but there was nothing to be read in his controlled expression.

'Mm,' she offered brightly. 'We'd have both been bitten to death by midges outside anyway.'

The restaurant was small and low-ceilinged, its furnishings softened with the patina of gentle aging. She could well understand why it was popular, she reflected, looking appreciatively around her.

The restaurant had a small private bar, but when she refused Luke's offer of a pre-dinner drink they were quickly ushered to their table. A good one, Natasha noticed, with a view of the river and yet out of sight of the people eating outside.

She studied her menu in silence, sharply aware of the speculative glances Luke was attracting from most of the female diners. She couldn't blame them. He was well worth looking at, and she after all shared their vulnerability to his good looks.

Their waiter was hovering expectantly; she returned her attention to the menu, choosing a trout mousse, followed by salmon as her main course.

'I think I'll have the same,' Luke agreed, asking her if she had any preference as to wine.

She shook her head. She had no real taste for alcohol, and said as much.

'Mineral water, then, I think, for my guest,' he told the wine waiter, selecting a bottle of wine for himself.

Now that she was with him, she felt ridiculously self-conscious...almost as awkward as a teenager, and yet during her months in Florence she had dined with some of Florence's most notorious flirts without so much as a qualm.

But then she had never been vulnerable to them in the way that she was to Luke.

'Tell me something about your work...how you first became interested in it,' he invited her over their first course.

Obediently she did so, admitting to herself how flattering it was to have his attention focused on her, to be discussing with him a world in which they both shared an interest, albeit on different levels.

'What about you?' she asked him. 'I know that you travelled a great deal before you started painting.'

Tactfully she didn't say just how she had gained that knowledge, nor that Emma had been scathingly acidic about his morals and lifestyle.

'I didn't travel, I worked my way around the world,' he contradicted her flatly, ignoring her tact. 'And if you know that, then I'm sure you know why. In fact, I comprehend from your remarks earlier on today that someone has furnished you already with a potted history of my life...or at least of the less appealing aspects of it.'

Caught in the act of breaking a piece of bread, Natasha discovered that her hands were trembling and that the soft roll was being crumbled to nothing while she fought to conceal her distress and her compassion.

'I'm sorry,' she apologised softly. 'I shouldn't have said what I did earlier.'

'Don't apologise. You had every right to voice your feelings and thoughts, unappetising though I found them. No one likes being brought face to face with aspects of their personality they'd rather not recognise. I might not agree with all of your accusations, but certainly there was enough truth in them to make me——'

He broke off abruptly, all the colour suddenly leaving his face as he stared at someone out of Natasha's view. Unable to stop herself, she turned round to see what had caused the shock etched into his features.

An older couple were dining at a table several feet away from them, the man silver-haired, expensively dressed, slightly portly in a way that suggested both wealth and self-importance, his female companion younger, but not young. In her fifties perhaps...unless that too smooth complexion, and too taut skin was the result of the surgeon's knife rather than nature. Suspecting that it probably was, Natasha studied them discreetly, unable to see what it was about them that had had such a profound effect on Luke. The woman's clothes were a trifle youthful and close-fitting for someone of her age perhaps, her laughter too high and girlish, her flattering concentration on her companion hinting perhaps at desperation rather than delight, but why that should cause Luke to look as though he had virtually seen a ghost she had no idea.

As she looked back at him, anxiously she saw him lift his wine glass to his mouth and virtually drain the contents. His hand was shaking slightly, and Natasha only just managed to hold back the exclamation of concern springing to her lips.

He had barely touched his trout, she recognised, and he barely touched the main course that followed it either, although he emptied the bottle of wine.

Throughout the meal, while he contrived to talk to her, she was conscious that his real attention was on the couple seated behind her. Much as she longed to ask him what was wrong, she felt unable to do so, and when at last they got up and left the restaurant she was conscious of a sense of relief, almost as though she had been holding her breath, waiting for something unpleasant to happen. She had refused a sweet, suddenly anxious to be back at the house and away from the restaurant, but Luke had ordered himself a brandy and to keep him company she'd accepted a cup of coffee.

Half an hour later, when they left, she was relieved to see that what he had had to drink appeared to have had no physical effect on Luke at all. Perhaps because she herself was so abstemious, she was over-reacting a little, she accepted. Certainly she had seen men drink far more than Luke had consumed tonight and still claim that they were completely sober.

His introspective, almost distant mood which had begun in the restaurant seemed to have deepened. It was almost as though she wasn't there, she acknowledged sadly as she walked with him out to the car.

And yet why should she feel rebuffed, rejected almost? They had come out to dinner as temporary colleagues, thrown together by circumstances. She had made it plain to him that her acceptance of his invitation was not a prelude to having sex with him, and throughout the meal he had treated her with courtesy and respect. Now if he was a little withdrawn, a little preoccupied by his own thoughts, wasn't she being rather foolish in wishing for something more personal . . . more intense?

Luke stopped beside the driver's door of the car, and then frowned.

'I think it might be as well if you drive,' he told her. 'That is, if you don't mind . . .'

'Not at all,' she reassured him, adding that the car was a similar model to her father's which she had on occasion driven.

Luke handed her the keys and walked round to the passenger door, leaving her feeling slightly hesitant and a little surprised by the knowledge that she had perhaps misjudged him a little. She would have thought he was a man who always insisted on being in control both of himself and of others, and yet tonight in asking her to drive he was virtually admitting that he was not.

Her frown deepened a little as she climbed into the driver's seat, adjusting it to suit her smaller frame, while Luke virtually slumped into the seat beside her before reaching for his seatbelt.

Natasha realised as she set the car in motion that her earlier surmise that the alcohol had not affected him had been wrong.

'I'm sorry about this,' she heard him saying indistinctly. 'Either that damn wine was a lot stronger than it ought to have been, or the more moderate way in which we all live these days has lowered my capacity for alcoholic consumption far more than I realised.'

He was massaging his forehead as though it ached, Natasha noticed, and she was sure that the grim set of his mouth was caused by more than the fact that he had had too much to drink. In fact she was pretty sure that it had something to do with the couple who had absorbed so much of his attention, but a reluctance to pry and be rebuffed for doing so kept her from saying anything.

The big car was a delight to drive after her own more workaday model, but she was glad that she had had the experience of her father's Daimler to familiarise her with the lightness of the power steering as she tackled the winding road that led back to Leo's house.

Throughout the drive, Luke sat silently staring out of the window, patently lost in his own thoughts. And those thoughts couldn't be happy ones, she was sure, Natasha recognised as she brought the powerful car to a halt in front of the house.

As she climbed out, she wasn't entirely surprised to discover that her body was stiff with tension, as though she had been locking her muscles against some kind of external pressure.

They went inside together, the coolness of the hall striking chill against her warm skin, making her shiver slightly and suggest, 'I'm going to make myself a cup of coffee. Would you like one?'

'To sober me up?' Luke derided, suddenly seeming to snap out of his private absorption to focus on her. And then, frowning suddenly, he apologised, 'I'm sorry. Yes, coffee would be a good idea.'

He followed her into the kitchen, making her aware of his height and physical strength in a way that was becoming achingly familiar.

As she switched on the bright fluorescent lights of the kitchen, Natasha reflected with relief that here in these mundane and unromantic surroundings she ought to be able to banish the rebellious thoughts and impulses that tormented her. Here, away from the soft, cloaking darkness outside, she should surely be able to close her mind to those unwanted memories of Luke's body against her own . . . of Luke's mouth . . . of his hands . . .

Her own started to shake as she prepared the coffee. Desperate to force herself to treat him just as though he were a casual acquaintance, she said quickly, 'I haven't thanked you for dinner. It really was kind of you.'

The explosive sound he made stilled her, her body suddenly gripped with sharp tension.

'Was it? Are you really trying to tell me you enjoyed it? Don't bother to lie, Natasha. It was a disaster,' he said harshly, 'and all because of that damned woman!'

Natasha couldn't move, dared not turn round, as she waited, wondering if he would tell her just what it had been about the other couple that had affected him so deeply.

'She looked so much like *her*—could have been *her*, in fact . . . if I didn't know that she's living in South America with her latest lover . . .'

'Her?' Natasha felt compelled to ask, but in her heart she already knew whom he meant.

'Yes, her—my mother,' Luke grated harshly, confirming her thoughts. 'Remember, Natasha? The woman who made me hate your sex . . . who deserted me and made my father kill himself.'

Whether it was the wine that had unlocked the iron control he placed upon himself, or whether it was the sight of the woman he claimed looked so much like his mother, Natasha had no idea. She only knew that the sight and sound of him in so much mental and emotional anguish acted on her own emotions like a powerful magnet, drawing her across to him, making her reach out automatically to encircle his rigid body with her arms, and to hold him tightly and securely as though he were a hurt child, rocking him instinctively against the comforting softness of her own flesh, while she reached up to smooth the dark hair off his forehead and murmur the age-old litany of comforting words that women had used as a placebo against pain since the dawn of time.

She had no thought for herself, for her own feelings or needs, no fears that her comfort would be rejected or mocked, only a deep, instinctive need to succour and heal. It was the embrace of woman for all that was vulnerable and mortal in man, completely non-sexual, completely selfless...a true giving of support from one human being to another.

'You were right in what you said this morning. I *have* been punishing your sex for her desertion...her broken promises.'

Natasha felt him shudder against her, and she knew sadly and instinctively that once this moment of intimacy was over he would resent her for witnessing what he would consider to be the weakness of self-betrayal. Whether it was alcohol- or emotion-induced or a combination of both, she had no idea; she only knew that he was suffering and that she must offer him comfort.

'It's over, Luke,' she told him softly. 'You must let the past and its pain go. Stop torturing yourself. It wasn't your fault.'

She knew, the moment he tensed against her, that she had found the centre of the emotional abscess that poisoned his life. Inside she wept silent tears for him, and for all the children who, hurt and confused by the complexities of adult emotions, believed that they were to blame for the breakdown in adult relationships, who took upon themselves the heavy burden of guilt and despair...who believed that it was something in them that caused their parents to leave them.

She had been lucky. Her parents had had a good marriage. She had had the benefit of the secure home which Luke had not.

'It wasn't your fault,' she insisted, ignoring the resistance she could almost feel emanating from his flesh, ignoring his unspoken desire that she stop. 'Whatever caused your mother to leave was caused by her own needs and feelings, Luke. There are women to whom the sexual side of their nature will always be paramount...more important than their marriage vows—more important even than their children. You can't blame yourself for the fact that your mother was...is one of those women.'

She felt him shudder, and then he said thickly, bitterly, 'So what ought I do? Accept the fact that she didn't love me?'

'If you can,' Natasha agreed steadily. 'For your own sake.'

She felt him move against her in rejection of her words, his voice stronger, harsher as he derided, 'What are you trying to do, Natasha? Play the amateur psychologist? Well, it won't work. You haven't told me anything I don't already know.'

He started to pull away from her and, as he did so, she lost her balance a little, falling against him so that he reacted instinctively and immediately, catching hold of her around her waist to steady her.

He was looking directly at her, and there was no way she could tear her own gaze away. Her heart started thumping erratically.

By some complex alchemy that she was way beyond understanding, she knew that he was going to kiss her...knew it and did nothing to stop him.

'Natasha.' He said her name softly, slowly, almost as though he were tasting it, and a *frisson* of sensation tingled down her spine, an awareness

of how much she wanted, needed to be held close
to him.

Surprisingly, when his mouth touched hers its
touch was gentle, caressive, without the sexual
domination he had shown her before.

It was a kiss more of need than desire, she
recognised in surprise; it was tender rather than
passionate, and, sensing his need, his pain, she responded to it generously, lovingly, wanting to ease
his anguish, to somehow make him whole again,
to restore to him what his mother had taken away.

# CHAPTER TEN

QUITE when desire overtook compassion, Natasha had no idea. One moment, or so it seemed, they were embracing without the urgency of desire, the next . . .

The next, Luke's arms had tightened around her, his body hardening against her, his hands moving urgently over her as though he wanted to make her aware of every pulse-point of his body. And all the time his mouth was moving on hers, caressing, arousing, feeding the hot, aching sensation that had erupted deep inside her body in response to the feel of his flesh against her own.

The sudden realisation of what she was doing, of what she was inviting, hit her, and she tried to drag her mouth from his, to lift her body away from its dangerous intimacy with his, but Luke stopped her, one hand tangling in her hair as he held her mouth beneath his own, the other spanning the small of her back, so that every movement she made to try and wriggle away from him only served to enforce on her the knowledge of his arousal. That knowledge proved too much for her own weak flesh. It had ached and yearned for this intimacy for too long, had fed itself on memories and dreams that faded into nothing beside the sharp reality of his proximity.

155

Luke's hand was still tangled in her hair, cradling
the back of her head, but there was no need now
for him to hold her prisoner beneath the passionate
heat of his mouth, no need for him to bite in sensual
demand at the soft curve of her bottom lip, tugging
erotically on its full tenderness, until she whim-
pered softly beneath the burden of her own desire
and clung recklessly to him, opening her mouth to
his possession in the same way that she knew she
had already opened her heart . . . and would surely
soon open her body. That knowledge made her
tremble, not in fear, but in a frightening awareness
of how committed to him she actually was . . . How
hopeless her belief that, somehow or other, by refusing to admit the truth, she could make it easier
for herself to shut him out of her life and her heart.
As though somehow she could actually prepare
herself for the time when he wouldn't want her,
when she would simply be another body he had desired and then forgotten.

She loved him . . . she always would love him. He
merely desired her. That should have stopped her.
But even as the thoughts passed through her
passion-dazed brain she let them slide away,
wanting, needing, aching for the narcotic he was
offering her, even while she knew that its pleasure
would be an arid one, that she would eventually
have to confront the truth and with it her own pain.

Hazily she wondered how it was that she could
so easily cast off her self-respect and pride, her
moral beliefs and ethics, and then, as Luke's hand
tugged her top out of the waistband of her skirt
and slid under it, finding and moulding the soft

curve of her breast, her ability to think, to reason, to do anything other than feel disintegrated completely.

She could hear someone breathing shallowly, quickly, each breath interspersed with soft sounds of need, but only realised distantly that it was the sound of her own arousal she could hear. All her attention, her concentration was focused on the pleasure Luke's touch was giving her, on responding to the hard demand of his mouth with passionate, almost fevered kisses.

Distantly she was aware of Luke removing her top and then her bra, unaware that she herself had begged him to do so, until she heard him whisper thickly against her skin, 'There... is that better? Is that what you wanted, Tasha?'

His voice was more slurred now than it had been when they left the restaurant, the words thick and unsteady, making her tremble with eager expectancy.

He was kissing her throat, while his hands cupped and caressed her naked breasts. She arched up towards him, moaning softly, and then gasping with pleasure as she felt the sharp pressure of his teeth raking the soft curve of her shoulder, making her twist and turn frantically against him, silently inviting him to repeat the caress over and over again until her body was alive with sensations... vibrating with need and desire.

She had no will, no needs, no desires, other than those he conjured up inside her, and when he lifted her against his body, arching her back in his arms so that he could repeat against her breasts the caresses which had already made her shiver with arousal and need, she didn't even hear herself cry out the sharp, anguished sound of intense desire.

But Luke did, and the pressure of his mouth increased until it seemed to Natasha that her whole world was concentrated on the tender area of flesh that Luke was drawing into his mouth, bathing with liquid heat and then tormenting with such rhythm and overwhelming intensity that the pleasure he was giving her was almost unendurable.

Only when he released her swollen, aching nipple did she come back to reality to discover, as he slid her slowly down his body until her feet touched the floor, that she could barely stand, so weak did she feel.

She was trembling from head to foot, aching with a teeth-clenching need that shocked her.

'Outwardly so very cool and controlled, and inwardly, so deliciously passionate,' Luke was saying softly in her ear. 'If I didn't know better I could almost believe that no one has ever touched you like that before.'

His hand reached out towards her breast, the pad of his thumb brushing her engorged nipple as though unable to resist its aroused allure.

'You're so soft,' he told her. 'So tender. I can't wait to feel how you respond when I taste you here.'

His hand left her breast to brush lightly against the front of her skirt, the merest pressure of light fingers barely touching the mound of her sex, but it triggered off such a reaction inside her that Natasha could hardly believe what was happening to her. His words...his actions...his intentions...all of them hit her at once, her body reacting to them so overwhelmingly that she had no defence against them.

The thought of his mouth touching her so intimately, which ought to have been so shocking, so unthinkable, had suddenly become a refined form of deliberate torment, a promise of pleasure, so desirable that she felt faint from the need it induced.

'I want you, Tasha.'

The words echoed through her body, increasing her aching tension.

'Let me take you to bed. You know how good it's going to be for us, don't you? We're both adults. Experienced. We both know.'

Instantly Natasha tensed, the husky, compelling words breaking through the bubble of desire blinding her to the truth. He thought that for her, as for him, this would be nothing more than simply another sexual encounter, and it was *her* fault that he thought that. She ought to tell him. She *had* to tell him. Panic clawed inside her as she realised that she had left it too late for any explanations...that he would not be pleased to discover now that she was still a virgin...that he was in no mood to listen to any immature outpourings of insecurity and need. And yet if she didn't stop him...if she let him continue...

She shuddered sickly, knowing what she must do, dragging herself away from him to say huskily, 'Luke, I can't. I'm sorry.'

For a moment he simply stared at her, and then as she watched she saw first disbelief and then anger darkening his eyes, and automatically she stepped back from him, crossing her arms defensively over her exposed breasts, suddenly aware that once again they were antagonists and not lovers.

'I think you mean you *won't*,' he countered acidly. 'Not that you *can't*. Punishing me, Natasha? Stupid of me, but I thought you were above those kind of games. Still, I suppose I should have guessed, realised that after all, underneath all that soft compassion, you aren't any different from the rest of your sex. Oh, you're perfectly safe,' he told her, watching with cynical eyes the way she flinched back from him. 'I'm not going to force myself on you, if that's what you think ... or want,' he added with unforgivable cruelty. 'I couldn't even if I wanted to,' he added brutally. 'Odd how even the sharpest desire can so easily die ... or be destroyed.'

He left her standing in silent agony and disbelief as he walked away from her and closed the door behind him. She stared numbly round the kitchen, blinking in the strong light, her attention focusing briefly on the crumpled piece of fabric that was her top, her hand reaching for it automatically while her brain tried to come to terms with what had happened.

She tried to tell herself that it was for the best ... that this way there would be less pain, less trauma, but her tormented, aching body refused to believe the panacea she was trying to offer it.

At some point she woke from an uneasy sleep disturbed by the sound of a car engine, but it wasn't until she woke up in the morning and went downstairs to discover that Luke's car had gone that she realised what that sound had meant.

Luke had gone.

She tried to tell herself that it was for the best, that in the circumstances she could hardly have faced him with equanimity. Even without his presence, her skin burned hotly when she remembered how he had made her feel... how she had openly and self-destructively responded to the way he made her feel. He had every right to feel angry with her, she acknowledged miserably. She ought never to have allowed things to get so far. She ought to have told him, stopped him...

But her weakness did not justify his total denunciation of her sex. She could understand that the rejection of his mother, followed by the suicide of his father, had been painful experiences for a young boy on the threshold of entering manhood, but surely with maturity must have come the realisation that not all women were the same, just as not all men were the same, that people were individuals... Unless... unless he had simply found it easier to blot out that knowledge, to tell himself that all women *were* like his mother and thus, in doing so, protect himself from further hurt, from the vulnerability that came through loving someone. And she sensed that, although he had not said so, Luke *had* loved his mother, which was why he had taken her desertion so badly. It was easy to understand how a young and impressionable boy might have reacted, might have told himself that all women were the same, and how the man that child had grown into would go on telling himself the same thing because believing it made him feel safe, inviolate.

It was not his fault that he should feel the way he did any more than it was hers that she should be unfortunate enough to love him.

What was his fault and hers was that both of them, knowing how diametrically opposed their beliefs and needs were, had allowed themselves to be carried away by that destructive surge of sexual desire, which both of them knew could only lead one way.

Yes, it was best that he had gone, but that did not stop her from wandering helplessly around the gallery, compulsively touching the things she knew he must have touched...the crates...the paintings...letting her fingers move blindly over them as though in doing so they could give back to her their memories of his hands moving on them, in the same faultless, dangerous way her body had recorded the sensations he had conjured up within it, playing and replaying them until she was so sensitised by her memories, so aware of the shocking intensity of her own need that she ached to be able to close her mind and body against him. To forget that she had ever known he existed.

Her aunt and Leo returned while she was still working at the house, both of them so obviously bursting with happiness that Natasha was not surprised when Leo announced proudly that Helen had agreed to marry him.

'Of course, he's only marrying me so that he'll get a cheap gardener-cum-housekeeper,' Helen teased, but the look in her eyes when she looked at him totally belied any real belief in her words. That they were deeply and sincerely in love was obvious and, while she was thrilled for them, at the same time Natasha was appalled to discover that she had to look away from them because of the weak, selfish tears clouding her eyes.

Leo insisted on opening a bottle of champagne so that their engagement could be toasted, and, although she tried to respond cheerfully to their excitement, at the first moment she got Natasha escaped to her own room.

How selfish of her, to allow her own feelings to shadow someone else's joy. She only hoped that neither of them had noticed how difficult it had been for her to smile and join in their pleasure, even while she was truly pleased for them.

When her aunt knocked briefly on her bedroom door and called out her name, Natasha got up to let her in.

'What's wrong?' Helen asked quietly without preamble. 'Or can I guess? Leo has just told me that Luke Templecombe was here over the weekend. My dear, I had no idea. If I had . . . Leo seems to think that Luke must have left in something of a hurry. Apparently he was to have hung Leo's paintings in the gallery, but all he seems to have done is uncrate them. Leo seems to think he must have been called back to London on urgent business. He said something about Luke being commissioned to do a portrait of one of the Royals.'

'He left last night,' Natasha told her, and then, unable to hold back her grief, she poured it all out:

her love for Luke, her discovery of the contempt and dislike he harboured for her sex, his belief that she, like him, was sexually experienced and that because of that she would be willing to enter into an arid, meaningless sexual relationship with him.

'Even if I were what he thought of me, it wouldn't make any difference. I still wouldn't want him on those terms. I couldn't...' She shuddered, knowing how easily she could, knowing how frighteningly easy it would have been for her to let go of her cherished beliefs, how frighteningly easy to give in, not to Luke, but to her own need, her own love. 'A self-destructive love,' she told Helen, painfully, intent on revealing every nuance of her own despair, admitting that she was as much to blame for Luke's departure as he was himself, not seeking to hide from her aunt her own role in what had happened.

'It was my fault. I allowed him to think...to believe...'

'Natasha, he's an experienced man,' her aunt pointed out gently. 'He must have seen...have realised.'

'No,' Natasha denied, gulping emotionally, unable to lay bare that final self-betrayal, to disclose that her reactions to him, her response to him had not been that of a woman who was sexually unawakened or hesitant.

'My dear, I'm so sorry. If there's anything I can do...'

'There isn't,' Natasha told her, biting hard on her bottom lip. 'I've just got to learn to live with it. No one asked me to fall in love with him, Helen,' she said painfully, 'least of all Luke himself. I knew right from the start just what he wanted from me. I told myself I could deal with it. I even told myself that I was being honest with myself, but it wasn't true. I realise now that part of me kept on hoping for some kind of adolescent miracle. You know the sort of thing—that he would look at me, and that everything would change... that he wouldn't just want me but that he would love me as well.'

She heard her aunt sigh and said thickly, 'Yes. Ridiculous, I know... stupid as well. Especially when I've always prided myself on my common sense, on my ability to control my emotions.'

'All of us are vulnerable when we love,' her aunt pointed out gently. 'Men as well as women. It sounds to me as though your Luke is frightened to death of allowing himself to love anyone.'

*Her* Luke. Natasha felt the aching tug of pain arch through her. If only he were her Luke.

'It's too easy to make excuses for him, to say that his mother's rejection allows him to behave the way he does, as though he's still a child and not a man.'

'I agree, and to be quite frank with you, darling... even if he could bring himself to say he cared about you, I shouldn't like to see you get involved with him.'

'There's no chance of that,' Natasha told her grimly. 'He's probably even managed by now to forget that I ever existed. After all, why should he remember?'

Her aunt sighed, getting up and patting her hand commiseratingly.

'If there's anything Leo and I can do...'

'Nothing,' Natasha assured her, 'other than forgive me for being such a selfish misery. I am thrilled about your engagement. When's the wedding to be?'

'December. There's no real need for us to wait that long, but the house should be finished by then. Leo wants us to have a proper wedding, as he calls it, and I must admit I'd like to be married in the same church where I made my first vows to your uncle. It sort of completes the circle, if you know what I mean, and besides, your mother would never forgive me if we opted for a quiet little ceremony. She and Leo are rather alike in both enjoying a little pomp and circumstance.'

Natasha laughed. 'Does Emma know yet?'

'No... I'm going to ring her tonight to break the news. I'm just hoping that Richard's work in his new parish will allow them to attend the ceremony, which is why we've opted for the first week in December.'

'Mmm. Well, if Leo's expecting to open the hotel for Christmas, as he told me he wanted to do, I'd better get myself off to Florence and order the fabrics we're going to need.' She gave her aunt a too brilliant smile and said shakily, 'If you want to look over the schemes I've chosen...'

'Good heavens, no,' her aunt assured her. 'That's your field, not mine, Tasha, and I know whatever you've chosen will be exactly right. Leo has been raving about you, you know. He's most impressed.'

'I've been lucky to get such a wonderful commission,' Natasha told her, her face clouding as she remembered the accusations Luke had thrown at her. Odd that they could hurt so deeply, cut so sharply, when surely by now she ought to be inured to pain, but every time she remembered was, like the first time, acute, heart-wrenching anguish.

Two weeks later she left for Florence, without having heard a word from Luke. Not that she had expected to. Nor hoped? Not even in the privacy of her own thoughts was she prepared to admit just how much she had hoped, or how unwisely.

She left for Florence, armed not just with detailed notes on the fabrics she needed for Leo's house, but also with various commissions and messages from her father, knowing that the time she spent there would be frantically busy, and hoping that somehow or other business would prove to be the magic panacea she so desperately needed to stop her thinking about Luke, yearning for him, aching for him.

Her mother had commented disapprovingly before she left, 'Darling, you're getting too thin. You look positively haggard. Doesn't she, Helen?'

Above her mother's head, Natasha and her aunt had exchanged a wordless look.

'I expect it's because she's working so hard,' Helen Lacey had dismissed, adroitly rescuing her, and then directing Natasha's mother's thoughts to another channel by commenting, 'I hope I'm wrong, but I rather think that Emma is going to make me a grandmama. There was a hint to that effect in her last letter.'

'Surely not so soon,' Natasha had heard her mother expostulate. 'I thought they intended to wait. At least, that's what Richard implied.'

'Richard may have implied it, but Emma obviously had other thoughts. And when did she want to wait...for anything?' the latter's mother had asked drily.

Emma having a child—not just any child, but the child of the man she loved. Something sharp had twisted painfully inside Natasha...something that was not envy, but rather a hopeless, helpless longing for something she knew could never be. And yet if she had not stopped Luke...if she had not insisted...she could now be carrying his child. She could now be looking forward to the compensation of having the child to love where she could not have the man. And she *would* have loved it, and in doing so would have shown Luke what? That he was wrong about her? To what purpose? Was she really so stupid, so criminally selfish that she would have allowed herself to conceive a child, knowing that that child would never know the love and care of its father. Had she really travelled so dangerously far down such a self-delusory road?

She was thinking of Luke when her plane landed in Florence, but then when did she not think of him? He had become almost a compulsive obsession with her, something she was unable to let go of, something she doubted she actually wanted to let go of.

In Florence she was welcomed warmly by those she had come to do business with, her expertise and knowledge recognised and admired.

She was, after all, her father's daughter, and in Florence, where generation upon generation had developed their skills in working and using the rich textiles she had come to buy, they well understood the passing down of knowledge and flair from one generation to the next.

Every night, every lunchtime found her eating with the family of one or other of her contacts, made welcome among them, and treated by most of them in much the same way they might treat a favourite niece.

She was beautiful, young and just a little triste— something that all Italians, but especially the Florentines responded to with all the passion and compassion of their Mediterranean heritage.

It was in the salon of one of her father's oldest contacts that she saw the magazine. It was lying half open on a sofa, so that when she moved to pick it up the first thing she saw was Luke's face staring back at her.

She dropped the magazine as though it burned, her face turning white and then red, her eyes blurring with emotion.

Her hostess, the mother of four teenage daughters and an adored and spoiled only son, saw what had happened, and discreetly led her young guest away from the others on the pretext of showing her some new curtains she had made.

Gratefully Natasha tried to pull herself together, to appear calm and normal, but when she left the house she heard herself asking awkwardly if she might borrow the magazine, her eyes avoiding the compassion in those of her hostess as her request was granted.

Once back in her hotel room, she devoured the article, drinking it in as though it were a life-giving elixir.

The writer was praising Luke's talents as a portraitist, hinting that he was now receiving Royal patronage, and asking him what had made him make the switch from landscapes to portraits.

It was all a question of growth, was Luke's response. A question of answering a need within oneself for development.

From the arch tone of the writer's article, Natasha guessed that she must have been attracted to Luke. What woman would not? She spent a miserable evening imagining the two of them making love—or having sex, as Luke would no doubt have described it.

She stayed in Florence for almost a month, working so hard that she completed all her commissions ahead of schedule and discovered some new sources of supply which ought to have thrilled her, but which only caused her to reflect that if she was not successful in her emotional life, then at least where her business was concerned she was not the same kind of failure.

She arrived home on a cold, windy day to find a message waiting for her from Leo asking her if she could possibly drive down to the manor because the first of the curtains for the bedrooms, made up from the fabrics supplied by her father, were now ready for hanging and he wanted her to be there to supervise this task.

Once such news would have thrilled her, but now she felt little more than a brief flare of surprise that so much time had passed. Was it really almost six weeks since she had last seen Luke? It was so fresh in her memory that it might almost have only been yesterday.

Luke...Luke...Luke...why oh, why could she not stop thinking about him, aching for him, loving him?

Why could she not do what she knew to be the sensible thing, the only profitable thing, and cut him out of her memory, forget that she had ever known him?

Because she was a fool, that was why, she told herself as she drove down to Stonelovel. She had learned from her mother that her aunt and Leo were both at the house, Leo supervising the work on his own private wing, and her aunt involved in the replanning and replanting of the gardens.

It was a relief to know that she wouldn't be in the house on her own. She had no wish to fall into the trap of daydreaming about Luke—something she was sure she would be tempted to do if she was alone.

Her aunt had never looked better, Natasha reflected, sitting sipping a welcome cup of tea while she listened to her enthusing over what she had managed to achieve.

Natasha had arrived half an hour earlier. She had been given her old room, as the guest rooms in the private wing were not yet ready for occupation, and she tried not to contrast her aunt's air of glowing happiness as she described how much progress they had made on the gardens with her own awareness that time, her life itself, both seemed to have become dragging burdens that were sometimes almost too heavy to carry.

It had been a cold, wet drive, and she had half expected to arrive to find her aunt's work impeded by the weather, but it seemed that nothing could dash her spirits.

'Once it's stopped raining—*if* it stops raining—I'll show you round.'

'And in the meantime, *I'll* show you round the house,' Leo announced, walking into the room to join them.

Later on, as she followed Leo and Helen from room to room in the hotel part of the house, Natasha could well understand Leo's pleasure in what had been achieved. All that was needed now were the finishing touches which would be provided by her fabrics.

Natasha found she was holding her breath, not wanting to go inside when Leo insisted on showing her the gallery, but once she had stepped inside it looked so different from the last time she had seen it that she managed to force herself to ignore the fact that it was here that she had been with Luke, talked with him, argued with him . . .

'Luke came back, then,' she commented huskily, unable to stop herself from admiring what had been achieved. It would be the easiest thing in the world to close one's eyes and be transported back to the seventeenth century. Even knowing that the paintings and portraits were in the main Victorian reproductions of paintings of the Elizabethan and

Stuart periods, it was easy to believe that they were genuinely of that period.

They had been hung in such a way as to mirror photographs Natasha remembered seeing of traditional panelled galleries of the Stuart period. Places where the ladies of the household would walk on rainy days, pausing to gaze down out of the windows, when the view inside palled, to admire the complexities of the herb and knot gardens set out below.

'Yes. He was here last week,' Leo responded. 'In fact, he——' He broke off suddenly, probably warned by a discreet look from her aunt, Natasha suspected, as she transferred her attention from the paintings to the other couple.

'It's wonderful,' she told them honestly. 'And when the fabric for the curtains and window-seats arrives ... Well, all I can say, Helen, is that you'd better order your Tudor court costume right now.'

She asked several questions about the paintings which genuinely did interest her, and learned that Leo had been collecting them over a long period of time, even before he had acquired the house.

By some heroic effort she managed not to mention Luke's name, nor to invite any kind of comment or information about him.

They spent the evening discussing the wedding. Natasha excused herself fairly early on, saying genuinely that she was very tired.

As she went up to her room, she told herself that she was glad that Luke had finished working in the gallery and that there would now be no fear of his returning...of their meeting, but the knowledge did not make her heart feel any lighter, nor did it ease the burden of misery she was carrying.

# CHAPTER ELEVEN

NATASHA had spent a busy morning organising the hanging of the curtains which had been delivered while she was in Italy. The firm who had made up the fabrics sent out a team of four from Bath to work under Natasha's supervision. She had dealt with them before, and the girl in charge of them was around the same age as Natasha herself, a pretty, plump brunette who, as Natasha already knew, was a bit of a daydreamer, inclined to see everything through rose-tinted glasses.

When she had finished enthusing about the house, she said enthusiastically to Natasha, 'You must be so excited about the wedding. It's a real romance, isn't it?'

They were alone in the gallery where Natasha had taken her to explain just how she wanted the Florentine fabric to be cut and draped once it eventually arrived. They had left the door at the end of the gallery open, and neither of them saw the man approach the open door, and then hesitate there.

'Yes, it is,' Natasha agreed.

'The wedding is being held in your home town, Mr Rosenberg says. Your mother must be so excited.'

'She is,' Natasha agreed. 'This will be her second wedding this year. My cousin was married earlier in the year.'

'I think it's wonderfully romantic. To have met almost by accident. If you hadn't been working here——' She broke off, flushing a little, and suddenly looking both flustered and excited as she stared at the door.

Natasha, who had her back to it, immediately turned round. The room seemed to spin dizzily around her as she saw Luke standing looking back at her.

'Luke...'

She wasn't even aware of saying his name, never mind the curious and half-envious look the other girl gave her, as the latter said quickly, 'Oh, heavens, I've just remembered I promised Jenneth I'd make some notes on what you want in here, and I've left my notebook downstairs. Shan't be a moment.'

Too bemused to stop her, Natasha couldn't drag her gaze from Luke as he stood to one side to allow the other girl to pass, and then walked into the room, closing the door behind him.

He looked different somehow. He was thinner, that was it, she recognised, greedily drinking in the sight of him, aching to be able to run up to him, to hold him and touch him.

His eyes, she saw, were glittering with a hectic, almost too brilliant fierceness, his mouth curling in a familiar line of anger and contempt, and her heart, which seemed to have stopped beating, suddenly started to flutter with frantic little beats that made her breathless and dizzy.

'So. You're going to marry Leo. I suppose I shouldn't be surprised. I ought to have guessed. But you see, Natasha, you really did deceive me. I really had begun to believe that you were different, that you were honest, that you would never lie or deceive.'

'I . . . haven't lied to you,' Natasha managed to tell him, her throat choked with shock and bewilderment. Why on earth did Luke think she was marrying Leo?

She opened her mouth to correct him and explain, but already he was sweeping on, refusing to allow her to say anything, his anger growing with every word he uttered, feeding on itself, until she too felt the white-hot heat of it infecting her own calmer emptiness.

It was like standing on the edge of a gathering storm, she thought distantly as his words, his scorn and his rage thundered around her until she had to shut herself off from what he was saying. Her face burned at the injustice of his anger, at his stupidity in assuming that she could ever commit herself to anyone other than him.

'What. . .nothing to say for yourself?' he snarled at her when he had reached the end of his contemptuous denunciation. 'Well, perhaps this will give you something to think about. Do you know why I came here today, Natasha? I came here to apologise to you. To tell you that you were right and that I was wrong. . .to tell you that I'd done some thinking and some heart-searching since I last saw you and that you were right . . . I was punishing all your sex for my mother's desertion . . . and more . . . I came to recognise that the reason I wouldn't let myself make any emotional contact with a woman was because I was frightened, terrified of being hurt again the way my mother hurt me.

'I came here to tell you all of that, Natasha, and to ask you if you and I could begin again. Make a fresh start. If you could perhaps teach me a little of your compassion, your generosity...if somehow or other we could find a way of making something out of whatever it is between us. And what do I find? I find that the woman who had lectured me so earnestly, so emotionally, the woman I had at last managed to let myself believe in, is nothing but a sham. God, at least my mother was honest in her rejection. At least she didn't pretend.'

He had been standing half a dozen yards or so away from her, but now, as she turned towards him with dazed, shocked eyes that focused helplessly on his face, he closed that gap between them, taking hold of her so ruthlessly that there wasn't time for her to escape him.

'You wanted me,' he whispered rawly. 'You still want me.'

'No.'

Her denial was meant more as a plea that he listen, that he allow her to explain than a contradiction of his accusation, but either he did not understand that, or he chose to misinterpret it, because as she pleaded breathlessly to be released his hands gripped her wrists and he hauled her against his body. She could feel the heat coming off it, the anger...the arousal.

He kissed her once, a fierce, contemptuous pressure of his mouth on hers that bruised and punished, and then again, equally fiercely, but this time with a compulsive raw desire that made her tremble weakly against him, her body sagging against the heat of his, her mouth instinctively softening, giving.

She heard him groan, a savage, angry sound that echoed her own frustration and need. His hands moulded her body, shaping it against his own, running over it with angry, restless movements that conveyed his need and his resentment of it.

One hand gripped the back of her neck, burrowing into her hair, the pressure of his kiss forcing her head back so that her body grew taut like a bow. His other hand spanned the base of her spine, pushing her against him, moving her in a shockingly open simulation of the physical act of sexual possession.

Somewhere deep inside her she felt shock, anger, and self-contempt, but overruling any kind of logical and civilised emotion was her own fiercely compulsive need to respond to him as aggressively and wantonly as he was doing to her. One part of her shockingly almost gloried in the knowledge that, even while he claimed he hated and despised her, he still wanted her. She discovered that she liked that, with a stab of shock bordering on that with which a lifelong vegetarian might suddenly and totally inexplicably discover a taste for blood-red meat.

It should have sickened her. Instead she found it euphorically exciting, as though in some way by arousing this anger, this need, this compulsive desire within him, she was punishing him, hurting him . . .

Hurting him . . . She grew still abruptly. Hurting him. How could she want to do that? Because he had hurt her? Was that any real excuse?

He had lifted his mouth from hers. She focused on it and saw that it was slightly swollen and bruised, that there was a small bite on his bottom lip. She reached out and touched it automatically, frowning when her fingertip came away marked with a spot of blood.

'Yes, you little hell cat, you did that,' Luke told her thickly. 'And we both know that right now I could lay you down here on the floor and take you and make you scream with the pleasure of our lovemaking.'

Natasha had gone white, but she refused to allow herself to be beaten down by his words—not when she knew that he was equally vulnerable, more so perhaps, since she suspected that he had never before had to confront the kind of need he was now feeling for her.

Hardly knowing where the words were coming from, she heard herself challenging softly and recklessly, 'Do it, then, but I promise you this, Luke—it won't just be me who cries out in pleasure.'

She saw him go white as he released her and stepped back from her. On another occasion the shocked look in his eyes might almost have made her smile, but, now that reaction was beginning to set in, she was beginning to feel sick and shaky.

'My God, what kind of woman *are* you?' he breathed thickly. 'Does Leo know about this . . . about us? And don't tell me that he makes you feel the same way that I do, because I won't believe it.'

'I should certainly hope not, since Leo is about to become *my* husband, Mr Templecombe.'

Neither of them had heard Helen come into the gallery. Natasha focused on her briefly, frowning a little as though she barely recognised her. She could hear the exclamation of disbelief uttered by Luke. She could see the cool control of her aunt's face. Her own body felt as though it were about to disintegrate . . . to fall apart.

'Ah, there you are, Luke. Did you find Tasha?'

As Leo himself walked into the gallery, Natasha knew she had had enough. She made a strangled sound of pain, and rushed out of the open door, heading not for her room, nor even for her car which would take her safely away from Luke and his cruel accusations. She was hardly in a fit state to drive, and the kind of solitude she craved the most she knew she could most easily find in the neglected walled garden on which her aunt had not yet started work.

The paths were damp underfoot from all the recent rain; the air smelled green and fresh, the clean scent mingling with the richer, more fragrant one of the old-fashioned bourbon roses which straggled untidily against the walls.

She sat down on an old bench tucked away behind an overgrown corner.

She had been there an hour, maybe more, when the creaking of the gate opening warned her that her solitude was about to be destroyed.

She wasn't perturbed; she knew that Luke must have left long ago, driven back to wherever he had come from by the same intense anger which had brought him into the gallery in the first place.

She tried not to let herself dwell on what he had said to her, on how different things might have been if he had only realised how impossible it was for her to commit herself to Leo, to anyone else other than him.

She wasn't, she decided drearily, prepared to make explanations or apologies. Why should she? He was the one who couldn't recognise reality; who could not or would not see the truth. Whatever kind of relationship he had wanted to have with her, for it to succeed it would have had to be based on mutual trust, and that Luke did not and probably never could trust her had been made bitterly clear.

That kind of outburst, that kind of anger, that kind of sheer blindness could only be overlooked or forgiven in a man so deeply in love that the mere thought of losing the woman he loved caused him such intense pain that he reacted to it illogically.

And Luke did not feel like that about her. Luke did not love her. She made herself say it out loud.

'Luke does not love me.'

'Wrong, Tasha. Luke does love you, God help him,' Luke himself groaned.

She turned her head in disbelief and saw that he was standing less than three feet away from her, looking both unbearably haggard and ridiculously boyish at the same time.

'No, please, let me stay... apologise... explain. God knows, if you listened to me from now until the end of time I doubt I could apologise in full. Helen has told me everything.'

'Everything?' She frowned at him, rather like a child trying to understand an adult. 'You mean she's told you that she's marrying Leo?'

'She has told me that, and much, much more. Do you mind if I sit down?'

He sat down on the bench next to her, and Natasha instinctively edged away from him. She was too vulnerable to him even now.

'Tasha, why didn't you tell me how wrong I was about you? Why did you let me think that——?'

'I was available and sexually experienced,' she flashed at him. 'You know why, Luke. It was to protect Emma. She was afraid you would prevent Richard from marrying her.'

'What? How on earth could I have done that? Even if I had wanted to, it's plain that he's besotted with her.'

'You told me yourself you didn't think they were well matched, and Emma heard you telling Richard's mother that the wedding could be called off.'

'By Emma, not Richard. Look, your aunt's told me everything. And I can't say that any of it has exactly endeared Emma to me. Forcing you into that kind of situation. Has she no sense . . . have neither of you? You do realise how close I came that very first night to . . .'

'To what? Seducing me, in my parents' garden?' She allowed her disbelief to colour her voice, shading it with scorn and bitterness. 'Oh, surely not?'

'You don't believe me. You've affected me like no other woman I've ever met, Tasha, and I've met plenty. Do you honestly believe I react like this to every woman, that I feel like this about every woman, that I've ever experienced this kind of wanting, this kind of intensity before? It's a whole new territory for me, and, like any other animal, I find unfamiliar territory makes me aggressive and wary.'

'I don't know what you're trying to say to me, Luke, but really it doesn't matter. I think it's best that you and I forget we've ever met.'

'Better...for whom? Certainly not for me. I want you in my life, Tasha.'

'Do you? Well, I've got news for you, Luke—I don't want *you* in *mine*... Not as my enemy, not as my friend, and certainly not as my lover.'

She started to stand up, but when he said quietly, almost pleadingly, she recognised, 'Not even as your husband?' she sat down again, her body suddenly boneless.

'My husband?'

'That's what I came down here today to say to you. That I loved you and that I wanted to marry you.'

'To marry me? But——'

'I love you, Tasha. I realise now that I fell in love with you the moment I saw you, but I fought against it as all men do. Only with me the fight lasted longer and was far harder. Everything you said to me about my past and the fears I had brought out of it with me was quite correct. I was afraid to trust...to love. I was still blaming my mother, when, as an adult, I ought to have recognised...to have accepted...that she was probably as powerless to control her emotions and behaviour as I was mine. You were right when you said to me that for some women their lovers will always matter more than their children. It was my misfortune that my mother was one of those women.'

'And hers as well,' Natasha told him gently, putting her hand on his arm. 'I'm sure there must have been many times since she left you when she must have wondered about you and wished she had acted differently. It must be terrible for any woman to be torn between her lover and her child. She probably thought you'd be better off with your father. She couldn't have known what would happen.'

'It doesn't matter any more. I've come to terms with it. A little late in the day perhaps. And as for my crass stupidity in believing you were marrying Leo... Will you believe me when I say that it was jealousy, nothing more, nothing less, that drove me to say the things I did? I'd found out from Leo that you were coming down here. I'd been waiting, planning, desperately hoping that you would listen to me, that it wasn't too late...that you hadn't found someone else, and then to walk into the gallery and hear you apparently discussing your wedding...

'Put yourself in my place, Tasha. If our positions had been reversed, couldn't you visualise yourself behaving, if not as badly, then at least similarly?'

She could...so easily...so very, very easily. The mere thought of learning that Luke was marrying someone else, the mere thought of contemplating it was like a vice tightening around her heart, a physical ache of shock, rage and pain.

'We're both alike in so many ways—both intensely passionate, both intensely private people. We both cloak what we feel in an exterior disguise of self-control and coolness. I love you, Tasha. I can't make you accept that love, and I certainly can't make you accept me. I know that sexually I turn you on, but I'm not going to use that knowledge to pressure you. I'm talking about a lifetime's commitment, a relationship based on not just desire but on love, on trust, on half a hundred other things that I know damn well I've only just started learning about. I need you for that as well, Tasha. I need you to teach me how to love...not love...I've already learned that lesson—too well perhaps—but how to love others, how to show compassion, forgiveness. Will you do that, my darling? Will you help me, forgive me, trust me, love me?'

Even if she hadn't loved him so utterly and completely, Natasha knew that her heart must have been touched, not just by his words, but by the very real emotion he wasn't trying to hide. He would never change completely; he would always have that touch of arrogance perhaps, and certainly he would never find it easy to trust where others were concerned, nor to admit them closely into their lives.

Their lives. She smiled inwardly to herself, knowing that there had really been no decision to make. She loved him, and, while that could never have been enough with the Luke she had first met, *this* Luke, who was prepared to listen, to humble himself, to admit his misjudgments and errors... *this* Luke who could tell her that he loved her and lay bare his deepest most personal feelings to her... this Luke was a man she could trust as well as love. This Luke was someone with whom she could share her life.

'You know I can,' she told him quietly, and then added, 'It won't be easy, I know that, but I do love you, Luke, and if you love me...'

'I do. I might have been slow to recognise it, but once I did...'

'When did you?' Natasha asked him.

'That night we went out to dinner together. I think deep down inside I knew it before then, but that was the first time I admitted it to myself.

'Kiss me, Tasha,' he begged her. 'Show me that I'm not dreaming any of this.'

'Mm. I hope this isn't just a dream.'

'That's what you said to me the day you told me you loved me,' Natasha told her husband, laughing up at him. They were lying on their bed in the luxurious Caribbean villa they had been loaned for their honeymoon by one of Luke's clients.

'You're sure you don't mind, Luke...about being my first lover?'

'Don't be silly.' He picked up her hand and kissed her fingers slowly and lingeringly, watching with appreciative awareness the pleasure darken her eyes.

'I was surprised, I must admit, when Helen first gave me that pithy lecture on just how wrong I was about you, but I'd loved you before I knew there hadn't been anyone else and——'

'You...you weren't disappointed, then...the first time?'

They had been lovers before they were married. Luke had taken her away for a long weekend and had made love to her so tenderly, and then so passionately that he had banished all her fears that he might somehow find her inadequate, but now, womanlike, she felt a need to probe...to exact verbal confirmation of what she already knew.

'In what? Finding that I'd fallen in love with a passionately intense woman who'd had the good sense to realise that I was the perfect lover for her?' he teased.

Natasha balled her fist and pretended to hit him, protesting when he grabbed hold of her and rolled her underneath him. The tussle which ensued left her breathless with laughter, until she felt the familiar hardening of Luke's body against her own and the laughter disappeared.

'We're going to be late for dinner again,' she warned him as he kissed her.

'Who cares about food? I have an appetite of a very different and far more essential kind, don't you?'

She did, Natasha acknowledged. It amazed her that she could feel like this, respond like this, that there should have been this intensely passionate side of herself which she had never known existed until she met Luke.

'Hold me, Luke,' she demanded fiercely, whispering the words against his skin. 'Hold me and don't ever let me go.'

'Never,' he told her. 'You're mine now, Tasha, and you'll stay mine throughout eternity and beyond.'

## HARLEQUIN PROUDLY PRESENTS A DAZZLING CONCEPT IN ROMANCE FICTION

 One small town,
twelve terrific love stories

### JOIN US FOR A YEAR IN THE FUTURE OF TYLER

Each book set in Tyler is a self-contained love story; together, the twelve novels stitch the fabric of the community.

### LOSE YOUR HEART TO TYLER!

Join us for the second TYLER book, BRIGHT HOPES, by Pat Warren, available in April.

*Former Olympic track star Pam Casals arrives in Tyler to coach the high school team. Phys ed instructor Patrick Kelsey is first resentful, then delighted. And rumors fly about the dead body discovered at the lodge.*

---

# *Janet Dailey*®

## *Americana*

Janet Dailey's perennially popular Americana series
continues with more exciting states!

Don't miss this romantic tour of America through
fifty favorite Harlequin Presents novels, each one set
in a different state, and researched by Janet and her
husband, Bill.

A journey of a lifetime in one cherished collection.

**April titles**  **#29 NEW HAMPSHIRE**
               *Heart of Stone*

               **#30 NEW JERSEY**
               *One of the Boys*

# HARLEQUIN *Temptation*

## Rebels & Rogues

**Jackson:** Honesty was his policy...
and the price he demanded of the woman
he loved.

**THE LAST HONEST MAN**
by Leandra Logan
Temptation #393, May 1992

All men are not created equal. Some are
rough around the edges. Tough-minded but
tenderhearted. Incredibly sexy. The tempting
fulfillment of every woman's fantasy.

When it's time to fight for what they believe in,
to win that special woman, our Rebels and Rogues
are heroes at heart. Twelve Rebels and Rogues,
one each month in 1992, only from
Harlequin Temptation!

---